DEAR HENRY

Connor Wray

Holland House

ISBN Paperback: 978-1-910688-18-2
ISBN Kindle: 978-1-910688-19-9

Cover picture and illustrations: B. Lloyd

Cover design by Ken Dawson, Creative Covers

Typeset by handebooks.co.uk

Published in the UK

Holland House Books
Holland House
47 Greenham Road
Newbury, Berkshire RG14 7HY
United Kingdom

www.hhousebooks.com

Supported using public funding by
ARTS COUNCIL
ENGLAND

For all those who have earned the title of Dad

Dear Henry,

It's thirteen years this week since I last saw your face, I don't reckon it looks much like it did back then. I wasn't sure how to start all of this, I've had the words bouncing around in my head for weeks, months, so I figured the best thing was to just try and get something on paper. I suppose the first thing to say is HAPPY BIRTHDAY! It's great to finally be able to talk to you on a birthday. Well, sort of, but you know what I mean.

You don't know me, you did once, but you definitely won't remember me, like. I'm your dad. Your real dad. I don't know what your nan will have told you about me, if anything, or if you've ever even thought to ask about me. I am so sorry it has taken me this long to get in touch, mate. I never wanted things to work out like this. I mean, it is how things were meant to be, but you have to let me explain.

You were born 8th March 2000. 9 months is ages when you know you're having a kid. I wanted to have you there straight away, wanted to get you started with a footy as soon as I felt you kick your mum's belly. That was the same day that your mum, Jess Henderson, passed away. She died in childbirth because of something called PPH. I reckon you've heard loads about her from your nan and granddad and that, but she was an incredible woman, mate. We were married just before we had you, and it was the happiest time of my life. When she passed things got a lot harder for me, mate. I was trying to hold down a job and raise you, and I couldn't do both. Bills were racking up and the time off I was taking to look after you meant I had nothing to pay them with. It should say electrician on your birth certificate actually, in 'father's occupation', should have a look if you get the chance! You were spending more and more time at your nanny Lynne's house. They were the ones that first saw you smile. It was when that happened that it just sort of clicked, that I thought you'd be better off living there with them. I couldn't face the shame of admitting to them that I couldn't afford to raise you, mate. I also would never have been able to live with myself watching you grow up from the side lines, knowing that I'd failed you as a dad before we'd even properly got started together. You deserved better than all of that, mate, you'd done nothing to deserve the bad start I was gonna give you. So I faked my death. I moved far away, so that you could be raised properly, given the best chances and opportunities and that. Given a proper life. I swore to myself that I would never contact you until I'd managed to sort my own life out, and that day has finally arrived, I think.

I'm so sorry, mate. I didn't want to lose you and I have wanted to talk to you every day since, but I knew I couldn't. I don't really know what I expect to happen now, I just knew it was eating me up and I'd planned to tell you when you got to a certain age and well, like, now you have, so it was only fair.

If you do want to get in touch send a letter to:

170 Old Christchurch Road,
Bournemouth,
Dorset,
BH1 1NU

I look forward to hearing from you.
Happy birthday, little man.

4

Dear Henry,

I don't want you to think that I'm weird or anything for bombarding you with letters and that. I can't say I blame you for not getting back to me straight away. My last letter was loads to take in and it can't have been easy to read, I just sort of blurted everything out onto the page, sorry about that, fella. I just wanted to send another one so you know I haven't gone mad or anything, I do want to talk to you properly, I just had to get some of that off my chest first. I'm not expecting anything to come of this really, I just wanted to let you know that your dad is still kicking about and that he loves you and thinks about you. I'm here if you need me.

I also realised that I only signed the last letter as 'Dad', and obviously you might not want to call me that yet since you don't even know me, like. I don't blame you, not sure I'd ever call my dad 'dad' again if he walked out on me. So my name is Robert Henderson, or it is to you at least. That's the name your nan will remember if you tell her about me, but if it's all the same, mate, I don't think it'd be a good idea to tell her anything yet. It's up to you, obviously, what you ask her and that, if anything, I just think it'd be a bad idea for now. I know I put my address in the last letter, but just in case you've lost it or anything, you can write to me at:

170 Old Christchurch Road,
Bournemouth,
Dorset,
BH1 1NU

Would be great to hear from you.

Yours sincerely,
Robert Henderson

Moss Farm,
Sandy Lane,
Brindle,
Chorley,
Lancashire,
PR6 8PQ
13.03.13

Dear Robert,

I wasn't sure whether I should write back to you or not. I spent a lot of time thinking about it and have decided that you at least deserve a reply. Your first letter was an awful lot to take in and I'm very confused. There are lots of questions that I want to ask but now that I am writing this letter I can't really think of any. I haven't told grandma that you wrote yet, as I think it would be best for me to hear this from you for now. I don't know what is supposed to happen now though, will we keep exchanging letters? I think that is the best way to keep in touch, and it is a cute way to get to know one another. I would like it if you could write to me again.

I enjoyed my birthday very much, thank you. We had a small get together at the house and all the family came over. I got some new clothes and an iPad, which I am very happy with. Grandma baked a cake with jam in it and vanilla icing. It was delicious and I had two big slices.

Thanks for telling me a bit about mum, I would love to hear more about her, but only if you feel okay to talk about it, of course. I guess I don't blame you for leaving, it sounds like you had a good reason and that you really didn't want to. I didn't quite understand all of how I ended up with grandma and grandpa, but you can explain that I'm sure.

If it helps, I really enjoy living with grandma and grandpa. Well, I do most of the time; they aren't too great to talk to about the football – ha ha! They take good care of me and grandma cooks all the time so I am eating really healthily. Which football team do you support? It sounds like you really enjoy it.

I was glad you sent the second letter. You are right, it would be strange to call you dad straight away because I don't even know who you are. It must be strange for you as well though.

If you faked your death does that mean that you aren't really Robert Henderson? Or is that one of those fake police names that you get in films? Grandma and Grandpa haven't spoken to me much about you, and I never really wanted to ask in case I didn't like the answer. Sorry about that. Don't tell me your real name if it is a police thing, I wouldn't want you to get into trouble for talking to me. How did you fake your death? Are you allowed to tell me? I saw from your address that you live in a place called Bournemouth, is that really far away from Brindle? Where did we live before?

I will have to try and see if I can look at my birth certificate, but I think I will do it without grandma and grandpa knowing for now. I will tell you if it says that you were an Electrician. I don't know where it is though; I have never seen it.

From,
Henry

Dear Henry,

I was made up to get your letter, thank you for writing back. I think you're right, it would be good to get to know each other a bit better and this seems like a good way to do it.

I'm really glad you had a good birthday, an iPad? That's sick that, what sort of apps have you got on it then? After I left you and Liverpool behind I got a job working with computers, believe it or not, so I sort of know my way about all the gadgety stuff now. Might even be able to give you a hand or something if it ever breaks or anything.

I was made up to hear you like footy as well. If you hadn't already guessed, or your nan hasn't told you before, which it doesn't sound like she has, I'm a Liverpool fan (because I was brought up, not dragged up like them Everton kids – haha). I used to play a bit as well, but looking back I was never actually any good. An above average Sunday league player at best, I reckon. Do you play? I've just realised that I wrote about Everton fans and you might be one yourself, sorry if you are, I was only messing. I don't mind really, obviously you can support whoever you want, like. It's just one of them old Scouse jokes I think, something my dad used to say to me and that. It took me years to understand what he was on about, if I'm honest.

I am living in Bournemouth now, yeah. It is quite far away from you, to be honest. I was trying to get as far away as I could so I wasn't tempted to come back to you, or interfere at all, because I knew it wouldn't be right. I sort of just landed here, if I'm honest. It's a nice enough place, like, the people are all right even if the accent is still a bit weird to me. Then again, it's probably exactly the same for everybody here listening to my accent. It's right down on the South coast, so I still get to do a bit of fishing when I've got the time, which is alright. Funny, I always swore I'd never live down south, but if I'm dead honest I think the fishing here is probably better anyway, so it's not all bad. Has your granddad ever taken you fishing? I remember Norm being quite keen on it back when me and your mum were together.

We used to go with him and sit all night down the prom. Your granddad would bring 2 massive thermos flasks of hot water with him every time, just in case he'd run out of tea in the middle of the night. He was tea-mad, your granddad Norman. Your mum used to come down as well, but she'd be there for about 20 minutes before she got bored with the fishing and went 'to listen to the radio in the car' for a bit. She'd be asleep 10 minutes later on the backseats, before we'd caught anything. Saying that, I'm not sure I ever saw your granddad catch anything anyway. Couldn't catch a bus, Norman. He used to tell me it ran in the family, that his dad was the same, and his granddad. He used to joke and warn me not to get too close to your mum if I liked the fishing, said it'd ruin me, that I'd never catch anything again. Funny fella, your granddad. I remember one time we'd gone over to New Brighton because your granddad had heard from one of his mates about a school of massive cod that sheltered near the walls there. It was utter rubbish, like, we didn't see any cod all night, but he was always chasing leads like that when it came to fishing. It was about the only thing you could ever properly blag him with. Anyway, we were over the other side of the Mersey and your mum had done her usual and gone to the car to fall asleep, and your granddad was fuming because he'd managed to crow's nest his favourite reel. He was effing and blinding for about an hour untangling the thing and cutting bits off. Eventually he got his tackle sorted and baited up. He was still raging as he went to cast out though. He did it with that much force he threw his rod clean over the wall. Aw mate, I was cracking up on the inside, close to actually physically wetting myself, but I didn't want to laugh because of how angry he was getting, so there I was trying to disguise my laughing with this pathetic cough. Must have been one of the first times I went down with him actually, thinking about it. Anyway, your granddad is stood on the edge of the wall, and he's just watched his rod sink down, but he can still see the float on the surface can't he, slowly moving away from the wall. He watches it for a minute, looks around at me, kicks off his boots and goes straight down the steps to the water's edge. Jumps in, fully clothed, swims over to the float and starts pulling the line up until he's got the rod back in his hands. Must have been about 3 degrees that night and all. All I could think was 'fair play to him', what a nutter. He gets it out in the end and comes up the steps still swearing, honestly, mate, would make your ears bleed to listen to it. When he gets to the top of the steps and rests his rod on the railings, I'm not even messing, fella, there's only a little silver Perch flapping about on the ground, still with the hook in its lip. Mate you should have seen his face. I've never seen someone go from anger to joy and back so quickly, he was buzzing – 'look at the size of that!' he's shouting, then the next minute – 'stupid effin' rod, never catches anything when it's in my hands', and so on. I couldn't hold it in, I just started laughing, I was in agony from trying to stop my belly from

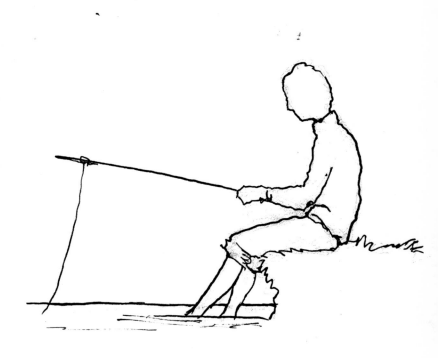

convulsing and I couldn't take any more. Dripping he was, celebrating over the tiniest little Perch you've ever seen. He throws it back once he'd calmed down a bit, and then sort of realises that he's been for a swim and he's sopping wet and it's getting colder because it must be coming up to midnight by this point. So he squelches his way up the road to find a phone box and calls your nan. Wakes her up in the middle of the night to drive over, through the tunnel and everything, to bring him some bin bags, because he didn't want to ruin the car seats. Nuts, he was. You should ask him one day if he remembers that, reckon he'd laugh about it now, like. Your nan still probably doesn't find it that funny though. Does he still do a lot of fishing? I bet he's still addicted to his tea.

I can't believe your nan has never even told you my name. I know she didn't like me much, but that's a bit harsh, I think. Well, I don't really want to speak bad about them, what can I say anyway? It must be even weird, all this, for you then, with you not knowing anything about me and that. Fire away, if you've got any questions about anything, and I'll do my best to try and answer them for you.

I'll wrap it up there anyway, mate. Hope to hear from you soon.

Love,

Robert

Moss Farm,
Sandy Lane,
Brindle,
Chorley,
Lancashire,
PR6 8PQ
18.03.13

Dear Robert,

Thank you for your letter. I couldn't believe the story about grandpa Norman. It was so funny! I would ask him about it but I don't want to embarrass him, plus he might ask how I found out about it. I will remember it and ask him soon though. I can't imagine him like that at all. He is so relaxed about everything now; I think it must be because he is getting older.

I thought it was an iPad, but I took it to school and somebody told me that it wasn't. I don't really know, but I don't think I'm going to take it anymore, I mostly just use it for playing games when I get bored at home anyway, so there isn't much point.

What is wrong with Everton kids? I didn't really understand what you meant; maybe it is one of those things that you have to be old to understand, like you said. I'm not an Everton fan though, if that is what you were trying to ask?

Bournemouth sounds very nice. I looked on the map and it is very far away, how did you get there? Does it have lovely beaches? Last Summer when it got really hot grandpa, grandma and I went to the beaches in Blackpool. It was amazing to just sit in the sun all day. I got such a good tan! I played in the sea as well, which was good fun, but I never realised how salty seawater is. We don't really have anything like that near our house, so it was a bit of a shock. The sea is very cold too; I couldn't stay in it for long. We saw some people fishing near the pier and grandpa Norman pointed them out to me, but he didn't do any himself. I think he must have stopped fishing now, maybe grandma got sick of having to pick him up soaking wet – ha ha! I hope he never swears at me like he swore at the fish, I just can't imagine that from him and I think it would be a bit scary. All he did in Blackpool was sit in his deck chair and read his book. I asked if he wanted to play in the sea with me but he said it was too cold for him. He did paddle a little bit though while I played. It was okay though, I made friends with some boys who had come down for the day from Blackburn, at least I think it was Blackburn, so I played with them instead. I still text them to chat sometimes, actually.

Grandpa Norman still loves his tea, yes, though he drinks a lot of coffee now as well. I think tea is still his favourite. Grandma drinks almost as much as he does, but she has started buying these weird fruit and herb teas which smell amazing but then when you drink them they all taste a bit like hot blackcurrant juice, which just reminds me of medicine. I don't know why anybody would want to drink them for the taste. I think my favourite thing to drink is Hot Chocolate, especially when grandma has remembered to buy whipped cream. One of my friends at school says his favourite drink is beer, which I have seen grandpa drink before. Some of the boys like to go to the cemetery near the school and drink beer at the weekend, and some of them have it at their parties now as well. I haven't tried it yet, though, because I haven't been to any parties lately. Also,

I heard about one boy who had vodka, and it made him throw up everywhere, which sounds awful. I would hate to come home drunk in front of grandma and grandpa as well; I think they would be very angry! Do you drink beer? Do you like it? My friend Jack says it tastes like earwax.

Hope to hear from you soon, Robert.

From,
Henry

Dear Henry,

I wouldn't worry about the iPad, mate, some of the best ones you can get these days aren't the Apple ones. I'm sure your nan and granddad shopped around to get you the one they thought was perfect for you.

How is school anyway? You must be in what, year 9 now? How are you getting on? What did the kids say about the iPad, haven't been wrecking your head over it, have they? Because you know to ignore all that, don't you? Anyway, year 9 means it's GCSEs next year doesn't it? Do you know what you're gonna take yet? I remember doing my GCSEs, was ages ago now, like. You'll probably have a giggle at this, but I did Drama. I loved it as well. We used to have this ex-dancer teaching our class and she used to make us sing our name at the register, or tap it out to a rhythm, every single time. Then we'd get to the lesson and it was always a musical, every week. She was mad her. What's your favourite lesson? Mine was always French because the teacher never turned up, and when he did all we did was watch films with the French subtitles on, was always a sit off. Not that that's a good thing, like. I mean, it's important for you to listen in school and that, otherwise you'll end up in a rubbish job like me.

It was a shame to hear Norman isn't as into the fishing as he used to be, although the fish are probably just as safe now as when he was doing it every week, to be honest.

Your nanny Lynne's fruity tea sounds weird, sounds just like her to start on something like that though. It probably won't last, I wouldn't worry, mate. She loves a fad, that woman. You wouldn't catch me drinking that sort of stuff anyway. Regular tea for me all day, fella. That or a cold beer, which I do quite like, yeah (but I prefer tea). Don't go rushing into trying all that though. Your mate Jack is right to be honest with you, it does taste a bit like earwax when you first drink it. At your age there's not really any point in drinking alcohol anyway. I started drinking when I was a bit older than you and it just kept making me sick. Make sure you're careful with it when you do give it a go, like, 'cause I reckon you're right, your nan and granddad wouldn't be impressed if you got in and you were drunk. Especially seeing as you're only 13. Swear kids are getting older earlier these days, especially with you saying your mates are already drinking. Mad.

Right. I was trying to get through this letter without bringing it up, but I've got to ask you something. I didn't want to, because after your last letter I was worried about what the answer might be. I thought it might just be one of those things that came up naturally as we were writing to each other and that, but it hasn't yet, and I think it's best if we just get it out into the open so we can get on with everything else. I need to know, mate, who do you support? I mean don't worry about it, there is no wrong answer really, whatever you say I'm sound with, I just wanted to know for sure. It's sound if you're not that into football as well, or if you're not as into it as I am. Don't go pretending to be anything just for me, that's not what this is all about! I think it's a borderline obsession for me these days anyway. I got in trouble at work on Saturday for having the match open on another tab on the computer while I was catching up with some paperwork. But then I dunno what they expect me to do, to be honest. If they want me to come in on a Saturday to sort out someone else's mess then they should expect that I'm gonna watch the footy, you know? What a game though! Wasn't bothered about getting shouted at to see Suarez grab a hat trick. I didn't think it was gonna be our day in the first half, like. Fancy going behind twice to Cardiff, what are they even doing in the Prem? It's definitely the English Premier League, and they're definitely Welsh. There's a Welsh Premier League and all, for that matter, why aren't they playing in that? And Swansea. Never mind. We're closing in on that top spot though, mate. I hate to say it as a Liverpool fan because it never works out and I always end up getting stick for it, but we are actually in with a shout for the league this year.

Enough about that anyway, best not to get me started or I'll end up filling reams with football chat. You must be on your Easter holidays by now? Have you got anything nice planned? Going anywhere with nan and granddad? What do you lot usually get up to for Easter? Loads of chocolate?

Love,

Robert

Moss Farm,
Sandy Lane,
Brindle,
Chorley,
Lancashire,
PR6 8PQ

26.03.13

Dear Robert,

I'm not so worried about it. I think grandma and grandpa thought they were getting the best one, or the best deal, it must be difficult for them to be certain. They aren't quite as into all of the modern technologies as much as it sounds like you and I are. I keep telling them about how slow our internet is, but they don't really understand that it can be slow or fast, they think the internet is just a thing. Like, you have it or you don't.

School is okay. Yes, year nine now, I think I'm doing all right, my results have been good so far this year. I'm in the top set for Maths and the second set for English and Sciences, but Mrs Riley (my Science teacher) says that I might be able to move up after the Easter Holidays. I wish some of my teachers just didn't turn up like yours used to! Then there would be nobody to tell me off if I just wanted to come home, or if I spent all day just reading in the sun, or in the library when it's cold like this week. Mr Derbyshire sometimes lets us watch videos in class, but they are usually old history videos or BBC documentaries in black and white, about Hitler, or the Vikings, or the Anglo-Saxons, boring stuff like that. I already have the form for my GCSE choices; I haven't filled it in yet though.

I know for sure that I want to take Spanish because I am quite good at it and I really like the people in my class. Although I think they split you into new classes once you get to GCSE, and we might get a new teacher too. That would be rubbish. Sometimes, in the really boring lessons, I wonder what school would be like or what would happen if there was only me that came in one day. Like, what if every other kid had eaten the same weird fish from the canteen the day before, on the one day that I had brought a packed lunch? It would be so quiet! I think the teachers would probably be much nicer to me if they didn't have all the naughty ones putting them in a bad mood all the time. I could get so much work done. Or what if I was the only human, and everybody else was a cat? Actually, then I would never get any work done, never mind.

Did you really do drama? That's brave! I always hated getting up in front of the class, Mr Boyce used to make us read out loud in English and I used to try and hide behind my book when he was picking people. I don't know why I didn't like it though, considering I used to sing. I sang in the school choir for a bit and I sang at the House Music competition when I was in either year seven or eight, I can't remember which. I don't really do it any more.

I have absolutely no idea what you mean by 'wrecking my head', but I looked on the Internet and it says it is a Liverpool thing for when people are irritating you? Is that right, because it doesn't make much sense? They weren't exactly nasty over the iPad thing, but I guess it was kind of irritating. One boy asked what it was and his friend, Josh Vickers, teased me about it not being a proper Apple one. I told him I knew that and that was the one I asked for because Apple ones are always breaking, but I only really said that because I don't like Josh. He has really greasy hair and once when we were on a school trip to Snowdon, in year seven, apparently he had a bit of an accident near the top because there were no toilets around. So nobody really cares what he thinks. I just walked away anyway and went to the Quiet Study part of the library for break time, with Charlotte, Jack and Molly. I tend to do that whenever I can't be bothered getting sweaty and dirty playing football at lunchtimes, sometimes it is so much nicer to just go and chat with them instead. I only really play football when Jack does, but he's pretty much stopped now because the boys in the year above used to tease him for how he ran and the way he kicks the ball. They used to call him 'crow' whenever they saw him because they said his feet turned inwards, but Jack says it's just more comfortable for him to play that way so I don't really see what the problem is. Jack reckons that Jordan Henderson, (he's a Liverpool player, isn't he?) runs a bit like he does, but then Jack is a United fan so what does he know?

I'm not an Everton fan, so you don't have to worry about that anymore! I'm a Burnley fan because of my friend from primary school, John McAfee. I hope Burnley is okay with you? His dad used to take him to all of the Burnley games before he died, and I got to go with them a few times. It was really good fun. Did you ever go and watch Liverpool play when you lived there? Does Bournemouth have a football team? I can see what you mean about Suarez, he is scoring a lot of goals this year! I had never noticed that there were Welsh teams in the English leagues, but now you mention it that is really strange. I didn't even know that there was a Welsh league, but that must just be because it is rubbish. I think anybody that makes you work on a Saturday should definitely be letting you watch the football, Robert. You tell your boss that your amazing son Henry said so, and if he disagrees I will come down there and give him a piece of my mind. Ha ha, only joking. Could you imagine that?

You said you work with computers and apps and things, right? Have you heard of WhatsApp? I managed to convince some friends to download it because it doesn't use up all our monthly texts and stuff, now Jack, Charlotte, Molly, Joel and me have a secret group on it, where we talk about homework and put up funny pictures and stuff from online, it's really good, especially when Mollie puts all the answers up before I've done the homework.

Easter in our house is usually quite quiet. Sometimes we will go over to Auntie Jo's house, but I don't think we are this year. We all give each other chocolate eggs, and sometimes grandpa Norm slips a shop gift card or a £20 note into the box of my egg, so that grandma can't see it. I'm never usually allowed to eat any chocolate until after our roast dinner though, and by then I'm usually too full to want to eat any at all! How do you spend your Easter? Do you still get chocolate eggs?

From,

Henry

Dear Henry,

I suppose your nan and granddad are a bit older now, like, but I'm sure when they were our age they were just as down with the kids. It's dead mature of you to look at the iPad thing that way though, you're a good lad.

I can't believe you're in the top set for Maths! You definitely didn't get your brains from me. I used to try and sneak a calculator into the exams but I always got caught. That's how your mum first noticed me, actually, or so she said. Said she looked up when she heard me getting carted out of our Maths exam in our second year, had to sit by myself under supervision because I was trying to use my calculator under the desk. Great news on your Science as well, you definitely got your mum's brains by the sound of it. She was top set for everything at school, except for PE. I think that and Drama were about the only things that I got better grades in than her.

Mr Derbyshire? Is that really the name of your History teacher? That's a proper History teaching name that, isn't it? I can just picture some old fella with a handlebar moustache and a comb over, always in an old suit with elbows pads and that. I didn't know you could speak Spanish, that's amazing, the most I can say in Spanish is 'two beers, please', and I won't be telling you what that is just yet. Especially if your mates are already getting caught up with drinking and that. Singing as well? You definitely take after your mum. What made you stop doing it? You must have been all right at it to sing in the House competitions. They're the ones against the rest of the school, aren't they? We had a similar one, but it was against all the schools in the area because ours was only a small school, like. I used to play in the rugby and the football matches for our school in them. I always wanted to play for the cricket team as well but my mates used to joke that it was a sport for posh kids so I never did.

How have you got to 13 and never heard anyone say 'wrecking your head'? I mean, I know it's a bit of a Scouse thing, but your granddad Norm used to say it all the time. Yeah it just means annoying you, sounds to me like there's a couple of kids you don't get on with very well, or at least that there're a few that are a bit mouthy, like. Just ignore them, mate. I'll tell you what my dad used to tell me: 'Never argue with idiots, mate. They'll drag you down to their level and then beat you with experience'. Just tell a teacher the next time they're getting on your nerves. If all else fails, there's nothing wrong with a giving someone a fat lip if they really deserve it, just make sure you don't do it so you get in trouble for it. I never said that though, if anyone asks, and you shouldn't hit people, anyway. Violence doesn't really get you anywhere, like, but, it can be handy now and then to just give someone a smack if they won't shut up. Not that I'm saying you should or anything.

You should tell your mate Jack that it doesn't matter how he runs if he plays all right. Tell him about me and the cricket as well, I regret that now, like. Nothing shuts people up like banging in a hat-trick, or throwing those last-ditch tackles in, especially on the playground.

I'm not gonna lie to you, my mate, but I was made up to hear you're a Burnley fan. Not as made up as if you were a red as well, but you can't get everything right (I'm only messing). I had a horrible feeling that living as close to

Manchester as you do that you might have been sucked in by the United or City fans in your school or something. Not that it would have mattered like, you know, it's just, well, Burnley is better, isn't it? They're doing okay in the Championship as well, that Charlie Austin looks a player, and that Ings actually. Sad about your mate's dad though, do you still go the games with him much? Mate, I used to watch Liverpool every week. Well, I did while we could afford it, like. The hardest part of leaving the city, besides leaving you behind obviously, was knowing I wouldn't be able to sit on the Kop any more. Even though you're a Burnley fan, you should try and get to Anfield for that. Go and sit in the Kop for a game, it's a special place, fella. If you go back through all the most famous games until you were born, I was at them all. Took a bit of a risk even after you were born, actually, back in 2005. You won't remember it, like, but Liverpool won the Champion's League that year. The semi-finals were against Chelsea and I wasn't gonna miss them, it'd been 20 years since we'd been that close, so I knew I had to get there. I couldn't get a ticket to the first leg at Stamford Bridge, but it ended 0-0 so I wasn't too bothered about that one, I knew it'd all come down to that Anfield game anyway. I couldn't risk coming up to the city though, in case someone recognised me. I'd only been away about two years or so at that point so it wouldn't have been worth it. I did the unthinkable, mate. I only went and got myself a ticket for the away end. I had to get a coach all the way up to Liverpool that was full of Chelsea fans. I hated every minute of it. Had to go in my plainest gear as well so that nobody would think I was a Liverpool fan, and sat amongst them trying not to show I was getting excited every time we went forward. The abuse they gave the referee when he gave that Garcia goal, I've never heard anything like it. Can't repeat a word of it in letters to you, obviously, it was disgusting, but I wasn't bothered. I was jumping up and down with the rest of the Chelsea fans who were launching the abuse, but I was just screaming. Funny now like, looking back I must have looked like I was off my head, but I knew I couldn't celebrate properly, so all I could do was jump and scream. I've never heard an atmosphere like that, mate, and then Gudjohnsen goes clear in the 96th minute and puts it wide, there was just a mad silence settled around the whole ground, both sets of fans. It felt like it took ages for that ball to go past the far post. Everyone just knew it was gonna miss but we all couldn't believe that it actually had until we saw it. The Liverpool fans all stayed to party once the final whistle had gone and I was gutted. I got escorted out with the rest of the away section, back to the coach and back off to London, all the while having to do my best impression of a cockney with his bottom lip sticking out. I got to see it though, so it was worth it. Getting to Turkey for the final was much easier, like, though I decided to take trains most of the way. Didn't want to risk flying, with my passport not being quite right and that, you know? Took a couple of days longer like, so it was just as well we got the result... in the end. One of the best nights of my life, that was.

Of course Bournemouth have got a team, they're in the same league as Burnley, you nutter. They've only just come up like, but that Eddie Howe is doing a great job. I've been to a few of their games, yeah, but it's not the same as being at Anfield. It's only a small stadium really, think it's only around 10,000. The fans are passionate enough like, and the whole town seems to support the one team, which is always nice to see, like. I don't mind watching them, they aren't in the Prem so there's no chance of them getting a result against Liverpool. I'll have to keep an eye out for their next game against Burnley now though!

I have heard of WhatsApp, mate, yeah, but I haven't got it yet. I suppose I don't have to worry about running out of texts though, so not much good to me. Sounds handy for you though, even if it is just so you can cheat on your homework!

Your Easter sounds like good fun. Who's Aunty Jo though? Never heard of her, like. She on your nan's side, is she? Never met much of your nan's family, to be honest. It's just like your granddad Norman to spoil you like that though. I don't think I've had a chocolate egg since I was about 17, mate, people tend to stop getting you them once you get a bit older, so enjoy them while you can. I do remember your nan's roast dinners though. Does Lynne still do her parsnips in that weird honey seasoning thing? The one she reckons her great-nan used to use and that she won't tell anyone the ingredients to? Was funny, that. I think my Easter will be a quiet one as well, to be honest, mate. There's some football on so I'll probably watch that, and then I've been invited round for dinner by a mate I used to work with, so that'll be good (not as good as your nan's, though). We'll probably take the dog for a walk along the beach or something before I head home.

Write back soon, my mate.

Love,

Robert

Moss Farm,
Sandy Lane,
Brindle,
Chorley,
Lancashire,
PR6 8PQ

17.04.13

Dear Robert,

I am very sorry I didn't reply to you over Easter. I started writing a letter back to you at the start of the holidays, but then grandpa Norman surprised Grandma and I with a trip to Ireland! We went for around ten days and Aunty Jo met us out there. Oh, of course, you don't know Aunty Jo. She isn't actually my aunty, that's just what we call her. She is one of grandma Lynne's oldest friends, and she comes to stay with us sometimes. She's very nice. But anyway, we flew into Cork and sort of slowly made our way towards grandpa's friend's house down in a place called Kerry, stopping off at some lovely places on the way. I was so confused at first, as I thought grandpa's friend was called Kerry and that's who we were meeting, but then we arrived and he is actually called Charlie, and his wife is called Claire. They live in the most beautiful house I have ever seen. It is in a place called Derreen Gardens and you can only get to it by travelling down this really narrow road on the edge of a cliff. The house itself is quite old-fashioned but it has a huge garden that is apparently owned by the National Trust, so I'm not sure how they are allowed to live there. It goes down some hills and onto the edge of a cliff, but you can follow the path all the way down and around these amazing gardens with loads of tropical plants and trees, and eventually you get to the sea. They've got two sailing boats tied up there, which we played on when it wasn't too windy. The sea is so cold to swim in, but it was really refreshing and so peaceful. It was just us in this humongous bay; which stretched out until it opened out into the sea. Around the bottom of the cliffs as well, there is something that happens that grandpa says is bioluminescence. I think that's what it is called. At first I thought it was a type of plant, but it turns out it is a strange fish-thing that gives off light on the top of the water. It's amazing, if you dip your hand in then the water around it lights up, I swear it's just like magic. Grandpa told me to dive in and swim about, and I was a bit scared at first, but then I did it and all the water around me was glowing and lighting up when I moved and it was so strange but so beautiful. I felt like I had magic hands and feet that could shoot off underwater lightning bolts. It was so cool.

Claire and Charlie have two children who live there with them, called Casper (weird, I know) and George. George is really little, eight or nine years old, I think, but Casper is the same age as me – he is very funny. I loved their accent!

Robert. You will never guess what I did... I WENT FISHING! Grandpa Norman suggested it one night over dinner, so the next morning him, Casper and me got up really early, before the sun had even come up. We found a flat bit on the rocks by the sea, where there were these funny little steps that sort of went all the way down until they disappeared into the water. We sat and watched the little orange floats bobbing up and down, eating bananas and drinking tea from grandpa's flask while the sun came over the top of the hills at the end of the bay. It reflected off the surface of the water so much that the float blended in with the yellow light, it was really hard to keep track of it. Once it wasn't so blinding it made the water so clear that you could see right down to the bottom of the steps. I was distracted watching some crabs that were doing this strange kind of swimming where they only had their eye-things above the water, it's the first time I've ever seen real crabs. While I was watching them grandpa Norman grabbed my rod and pulled it towards himself really quickly. He started winding in the reel and Casper ran down the steps to grab our net. I had no idea what was going on until grandpa flicked the rod again and a huge grey fish came flying out of the water toward us. The fishing line was so thin and difficult to see in the light that it looked like the fish was just sort of flying around our heads. Casper said it was a mackerel fish and I think grandpa Norman wanted to keep it, but Casper said it was too small so he threw it back into the water. I think grandpa must have gotten much better at fishing since you used to go with him, because he caught six mackerel that morning! I caught two but they were really small, and one wasn't a mackerel but I forget what it was called. We kept the biggest of them in the net, then when we were getting ready to leave Casper picked each of them up in turn and started smacking their heads against the rocks. I was shocked at how cruel he was being until grandpa explained it is the kindest way to kill them. It was quite sad really, because the fish haven't exactly done anything wrong, they were just unlucky I suppose. I felt much better about it all once I had tasted them though. Casper tried to teach me how to gut the fish in the bathroom sink, but I thought I was going to be sick after he took the bones out of the first one, so I let him finish the rest. Everybody was so impressed when we sat down to lunch and there was a whole fish each! It was delicious, easily the best fish I have ever eaten. That night we had a huge bonfire outside and Charlie invited loads of people over for a party. Casper stole two beers out of the big bucket that had them all in, and we sat by the bonfire away from the adults to drink them. Beer tastes horrible. I didn't finish it; I don't understand how anybody drinks it. Jack was right.

Oh, that reminds me, I already know how to say that in Spanish, it's 'dos cervezas, por favor', but you have to be careful how you say 'cervezas', because they say it differently depending on which country you are in.

Anyway, after being in Ireland I can totally understand why you wanted to live by the coast after you left Liverpool, especially if it was so you could keep fishing and eat like that all the time.

I can't believe you sat with the other team's fans for the semi-final, it must have been horrible for you. It's a good job you won otherwise that journey back to London would have been just awful. It sounded like an amazing game; I will have to see if I can find any highlights or something of it on YouTube. I found some of the final that you mentioned. I can't believe I hadn't heard about it before. 3-0 to 3-3 then penalties? No wonder it was one of the best games you've ever seen!

Don't be too jealous over grandma Lynne's roast dinner, I didn't get one either this year. Then again, I did get one cooked by Charlie, who I'm pretty sure works for some kind of food company, and that one was pretty good too.

Plus, I was in Ireland, so maybe you should be jealous – ha ha!

You said in your last letter that I got my brains from mum. Was she really clever? What did she work as? I would like to know more about her. Only if you feel like you can talk about it, though, I don't want to upset you.

Love,

Henry

P.S: What kind of dog does your friend have? My friend Jack (with the funny run) has a black one that looks like a wolf, called Benji. It is so cool.

Dear Henry,

That sounds like an amazing Easter. Never heard of your nan's mate, your Aunty Jo, but then I never really met much of your nan's side of the family. Your nan was always a bit hesitant to introduce me to them, I think. I've never been to Ireland, but you made it sound so good I might have to one day. I'm made up you got to see your granddad fishing, although I don't believe for a second that he caught anything. You did it properly as well by the sounds of it, getting up early and that. Nothing better than watching that sun come up over the water, feeling it slowly get hotter before you get blinded by the light of a new day. There's a strange kind of peace, that early in the morning, that I think you only ever get in those moments in that sort of light. Like you can see out into the whole world, everything that's happening anywhere, but it only exists between the cup of tea in your one hand and your rod in the other. That's what it's all about, mate, you can see what I was on about now, can't you? You're right and all, there is something so calm about being that close to the water. I don't think I could live anywhere else now, if I'm honest. I tried for a bit in other places but there's just something about that air that comes rolling in off the coast. Maybe it's the salt in it, or the fact that it's got a bit of foreign wind in it or something, but it's the freshest air you'll ever breathe. They've done studies now, you know, about where the happiest people live. They found that people who live by the coast are the happiest in the world, which I thought was a bit weird, how exactly do you measure stuff like that?

It's an odd thought that, don't you think? That the wind has come from somewhere else. Like it's travelled thousands of miles over oceans or deserts, just to blow cold against your face, make you pull your coat up that bit further.

You ate the fish as well, good lad. I'll let you into a little secret, I hate gutting fish as well. It's just dead slimy and you can't grab anything properly, plus the feel of the insides is horrible, so I'm not surprised you didn't like it. The best bit is catching them. Well, no, the best bit is eating them if that's what you're catching them for, but you know what I mean.

I'm glad you managed to make friends over there, the accent is funny isn't it? Takes a bit of getting used to, I reckon. Casper is a bit of a weird name, like, but he must be a sound kid if you got on with him so well. I say that, he seemed all right to me until you mentioned him robbing beers for you. You're a bit young for all that, aren't you? Still, if you didn't like it there's nothing really to worry about, I suppose.

Calm down showing off with your Spanish there, mate! I haven't got a clue what you're on about with the pronunciations bit. Lost on me, that.

Ah, where do I start with your mum? Yeah she was dead clever, mate. She actually wasn't working when you were born. She'd been off to uni for a few years and hadn't long moved home when we found out she was pregnant, so she said she'd put off getting into work until after she'd had you. She wanted to be a Weather Reporter, you know like one of the weather girls on the news? She did Meteorology down in Reading. I'd never even heard of the place until she told me she was going there. It's not miles away from London, sort of between there and Oxford. She lived in this weird little house that had the bathroom at the back of the kitchen and then another toilet built dead randomly into the cupboard under the stairs. She shared it with three other girls she met while she was down there. They were sound but they were a bit boring, like. I used to finish work early as I could on a Friday, go into the office to sign off for the week and collect my wages, then it was straight to the train station or onto the motorway to go down and see her for the weekend. I must have done that nearly every week, I reckon. Absolute pain it was, 4 hours there and back every Friday and Sunday night, or Monday morning if I could be bothered with it, or if I had easy jobs on. But I loved her, fella, so you end up doing weird stuff like that.

She had all these mad assignments for her course, like learning scripted weather reports and then getting all dolled up and reading it out in front of a green background while they filmed her. When I first saw her department from the outside I thought it was one of them dog training places, you know for like the dogs that go on Crufts and that? Turns out it was just a load of equipment for measuring atmosphere, pressure, rainfall, that sort of thing. Your mum understood what all of it did. I didn't have a clue. I used to tease her and get her to tell me what the weather was gonna be like for the drive home. She used to say that she couldn't do that yet, or that it wasn't the sort of stuff she was studying, or some other excuse, but eventually she'd give it a go and she was never too far off actually, now that I think about it. I know it's your mum and that, and it's horrible hearing about your parents in this way, but she was mesmerising when she was talking about her course. I never understood a word of it, but I used to be hypnotised watching her lips and the way she used her hands to explain things. Really pale skin she had, especially on her hands. Gorgeous, mate.

I went to her graduation with your nan and granddad. Me and your nan never used to get on, to be honest, and she really didn't want me to come with them at first. She's not one to hold back in saying stuff like that either, as you've probably already realised. Eventually I think she realised that I'd be an extra pair of hands to hold the camera and take pictures of them all together and she eased up a bit after that. Well, I say eased up, she stopped complaining about me going, at least out loud. I've got a picture somewhere from that day, actually, if I can find where it is I'll send it over to you. Only if you promise to look after it though! Saying that you've probably seen them all already. Once she was done with uni she came back home and moved in with me for a bit. She spent most of the week at Lynne and Norm's though, because I think she got bored being in our dingy little flat all day, plus she always hated cooking for herself.

So yeah I reckon you definitely get your brains from her, mate. I could fill pages just talking about her but I don't wanna just waffle on forever. It's up to you, fella, just ask if there's anything else you want to know.

My Easter was okay, cheers. I watched the football, but I won't go on about it in case I jinx this weekend. All I'll say is if you haven't seen the league since you got back from Ireland, go and have a look. Oh and if you get the chance, watch Gerrard after the game at the weekend. Funny, but inspiring, mate, I definitely can't see us losing that lead at the top if he has anything to do with it! I watched that then I went over to Sam's for dinner and we took the dog down the beach, threw the ball around for him for a bit until the sun went down. It was a pleasant evening actually. We went back to Sam's after that and just watched films for a bit. Nowhere near as exciting as your Easter though by the sounds of it! I didn't get to do any fishing so you definitely won there. When are you back in school then? Must be soon, excited yet? I'm only messing.

Love,

Robert

P.S: Sam's dog is a Golden Labrador called Kevin, which I've told her is a rubbish name for a dog. Think we're taking him out again this weekend. Jack's dog sounds dead cool.

Moss Farm,
Sandy Lane,
Brindle,
Chorley,
Lancashire,
PR6 8PQ

27.04.13

Dear Robert,

You have to go to Ireland! It is one of the best places I have ever been, I miss it so much already. You're definitely right about the coast and being happier. I was certainly happier fishing in Ireland than I am about being back at school in Brindle! Grandpa Norman seemed happier too, he must have been to suggest that we went fishing in the first place, he's never done that at home before. Then again, there aren't many places we could go fishing round here, so maybe that's why.

Don't worry Robert, it was just one beer and as I said I hated it. I have added Casper on Facebook now, so we are keeping in touch. He says that next time we go over there he'll teach me to play Gaelic Football. I told him I already know how to play football but apparently it's not the same?

I can't believe you used to travel four hours every week just to see mum. Why did you bother with that? Or were you trying to be all romantic, ha ha! It sounds like she was super-clever, I'm sure she would have made an amazing weather reporter. Can you imagine how funny that would have been for us, to have come home from work or school and sit down in front of the TV and watch mum telling us what the weather was going to be like? That would have been so weird, like she was always there in the room with us, even if she had to go really far away to do the weather reports. I think that would have been lovely.

It sounds like she had fun at uni, too. I think grandpa and grandma want me to go to uni as well eventually. I keep telling grandpa that I don't want to go because I'm going to be a fireman, but he says I can do both anyway and it will help. Maybe if I do go I could study Meteorology too. Actually, I always think it's really boring when grandpa talks about the weather, so perhaps it's not such a good idea.

Please do send the picture if you can find it, I would love to see that. I have seen some others from mum's graduation, I think, when I was very little, but none of them had you in. It makes sense that you and grandma didn't get along so well, because I don't think she has ever even mentioned you. It would be a chance to see what you look like too! It's been nearly three months since we started speaking now and I still have no idea what you look like. If you send me a picture of you and mum I promise I will send one of me to you. Of course, only do it if you think it is safe. I don't want you to do it if you think it is risky or you could get into trouble.

How did you and mum first meet? When did you get married? I bet that's a really sweet story.

I missed all of the football over Easter because of Ireland, and I haven't caught up yet because I was getting ready to go back to school, but I'll definitely have a look for what you mentioned. We're only three days into the new term and I already can't wait for Summer.

Your Easter sounds like it was very peaceful. Sam's dog

sounds really cool, but yes, tell him I said it is a rubbish name as well. Kevin isn't a proper dog's name! Does Sam work with you then? Is he a Liverpool fan as well?

Love,

Henry

Dear Henry,

I'm sure you could find a fresh water stream or something nearby that you could fish at. If you really want to do it again you should just ask your granddad, I reckon he'd be made up.

Gaelic Football is totally different, mate. It's a dead confusing game, that's all I know. I don't understand it at all but it looks brutal. They play it with like these mad hockey sticks and they're all massive like rugby players.

I reckon you'll understand a bit better why I drove to see your mum when you get a bit older. You do funny stuff like that for girls, mate, you won't know what I mean at the moment though. Funny you should mention coming home to watch your mum's weather reports, I had that same picture in my head when she first got pregnant. I doubt she'd have ever been that far away though, most of the news reports get done in a studio, so she would never have had to travel anywhere, I don't think.

You should try to go to uni, if you can. You've got ages yet, but your granddad is probably right in that you could do both if you wanted. Why do you want to be a fireman? I was still convinced I was gonna be a footballer when I was your age, that didn't work out so well for me, but you've got loads of time. If you do go to uni, Meteorology would be a good one, would definitely make your mum proud from wherever she's watching you now.

I had a look for the pictures but I couldn't find them. I think they might be in your nan's house, in the attic somewhere, so it might be worth asking her if she's still got them and to dig them out. I haven't checked any of the folders under my bed yet though, so they might be in there. I take it your nan never showed you any pictures of me then, if she made sure I wasn't in any of the graduation ones? I suppose I understand it being a bit of a sore subject for her, what with the way everything happened and that, but I thought you might have asked about me at some point. Even if you didn't ask, or you were scared to, it's a bit bang on that they've never mentioned your real dad to you. I get that she might not want to talk about it, but it isn't very fair on you. It's no risk to send you a picture from that long ago, I don't reckon. Don't panic about all of that either, all I mean when I say stuff like that is that I have to be a bit careful. There'd be no point in me getting away and leaving you safe only to go and get caught and not be able to speak to you any more. I wasn't so bothered about it before, but as you said, it's been a good few months now and I don't really want to lose this again so soon.

The proposal to your mum was a funny one. I proposed on her 22nd birthday. To be honest with you, mate, I only did it because I couldn't think of anything else to get her. The mistake I made was that I told her that though. Got down on one knee while we were at this place called Everton Valley, which she used to love going to, because you could see out over the whole city. She liked it because it wasn't the usual view, like from the waterfront and that. It wasn't dead touristy, she used to say. We'd been for a meal and went up there for a bit as we used to do, and then we walked down to get to the bit with the best view. I asked her if she wanted her birthday present there and then, and she said she did, so I got down on one knee and I was that nervous that I started with, 'well, Jess, you're dead hard to buy for and that, and I couldn't think of what else to get you, so...' she said it was the least-romantic romantic proposal she'd ever heard. I said it had better have been the only proposal she'd ever heard! It's a wonder she said yes, looking back. She loved it really, I think. The worst bit of the whole thing was asking for your granddad Norman's permission. He agreed, obviously, but only if I could beat him in a game of chess. I know, mate, mad that isn't it? Like I said though, he's a nutter your granddad. He never said why it had to be chess, but that was his one condition, so I had to give it a go. It took me 4 tries to do it, and I'm pretty sure that after the first 3 he just let me win. I think he just wanted to see how serious I was, because they were some awkward games at first. We just had nothing to say to each other. It got easier by the end though, we'd bonded a bit by then. Your mum thought it was the weirdest thing, how me and your granddad had suddenly just gotten obsessed with playing chess every time we saw each other. She didn't suspect a thing until I told her as well. She kicked herself, said it was dead obvious, she should have guessed. Just like Norm, to do something like that.

We hadn't really made any solid plans as to when the wedding would be, but then she got pregnant with you and we sort of had to speed it up a bit. Not like you have to be married to have kids, although don't tell your nan I said that to you. It was her that really made us do it, she's a bit old-fashioned like that, your nan. Comes from a pretty well off Catholic family, I dunno if you knew that? She always had a bit of a thing about me not being quite as refined as she wanted for her daughter. First few times I went round to see your mum at their house she'd make little snide comments like 'did nobody ever teach you how to use a knife and fork?' or 'Do you not say Grace in your house, Robert?'. The longer I was with your mum the more she mellowed, although she was fuming when she found out I was staying with your mum at uni on the weekends. She'd call your mum and rant on about how she'll end up pregnant to a man she had no intention of marrying. I suppose she was sort of right in the end, only your mum did want to marry me. It was more to shut your nan up than anything else that we got married, to be honest with you, fella. So we went for it, dead quick, handful of mates invited to the church at the end of the road, and the family obviously, and that was that. I'd sorted us out a trip down to Cornwall for our honeymoon, booked a caravan and that, and then on the big day your granddad surprised us with two tickets out to Barcelona. He used to spoil your mum just like I reckon he spoils you now. It was good fun that trip. I wanted to go and watch a Barca game at the Nou Camp, but your mum was having absolutely none of it. She said I went to enough games back home, I needed a holiday from it as well. In fact, I think other than the final in Turkey, which doesn't really count, that was the last time I went on holiday anywhere.

Your mum would definitely make me take a break away from football now, actually. I dunno if you've caught up yet, but I wouldn't bother to be honest, mate. Been waiting for us to win the league since before you were born, since I was younger than you, but it looks like I'll be waiting a bit longer now. Couldn't write it, could you? Gerrard, of all people. I suppose 1 bad game out of 38 isn't too bad, just had to be that one, didn't it? At least Burnley look set to come up, you must be buzzing, fella. Can look forward to some Liverpool Burnley games next season!

He? Ah, sorry mate, I meant Sam as in Samantha. She's a girl, but yeah I work with her. Well, I used to, she used to be in the finance bit of our offices, but she's moved into working for an advertising company now. I've tried telling her she needs to change the dog's name, I even told her that you said it's rubbish. He sort of suits it though, the dog I mean. He has got to be the dumbest dog I've ever met, all he does is sleep all day, and you can hear the snores from anywhere in her house. He's got a tail like a whirlwind as well. Leave anything on the coffee table and if he walks past it'll be all over the floor, up the walls, on the ceiling. That thing's dangerous, I swear.

Why is school rubbish anyway? Those lads aren't giving you grief again are they? Tell someone if they are, mate.

Love,

Robert

Moss Farm,
Sandy Lane,
Brindle,
Chorley,
Lancashire,
PR6 8PQ

10.05.13

Dear Robert,

That's a good point; I think I will ask him if we can go fishing over the half term holidays.

I sort of see what you mean about doing weird stuff for girls, actually. There's this one girl in school who sits in front of me in Science who I always get told off for chatting to. That reminds me, I forgot to say, Mrs Riley decided I could go up a set, so now I am in top set for Science as well! Anyway, I've been getting told off because I keep winding this girl up in front of me. Just stupid stuff really, poking her, whispering to her so quietly that she has to turn around to hear me and then she gets into trouble for it. On Monday I got her book and swapped it with mine, so that she did all the work in mine and I did rubbish work on purpose in hers, then at the end of the lesson I told her and swapped them back over. She sort of finds it funny, but then I get told off for irritating her all the time. It's funnier because I never do stuff like that with my boy friends. Not boyfriends, my friends who are boys. You know what I mean. With them it's always just shouting or throwing stuff around, or fighting when the teacher isn't looking. When I'm messing about with the girls I have to think about it a bit more. At lunchtimes she sits in the same quiet study place that me, Mollie and Jack sometimes go to sit in, but she is always sat giggling with her friends who I don't really know, so I never really get the chance to talk to her properly. My music teacher said I should stop flirting with her and just talk to her like an adult, but I'm blatantly not flirting with her, so that wasn't very helpful.

I will see about university in the future I think. I don't really know why I want to be a fireman. Probably because it looks like good fun using the pole and the hose all day! Plus they have those huge axes, which are pretty cool.

It's a shame you couldn't find those pictures; I would ask grandma but obviously I don't want her to know I'm sending letters to you. She knows I'm sending letters to somebody, but I've told her it's a pen pal project for school and she seemed fine with that. I haven't ever been shown pictures of you, sorry. Why is that? It's not like you did anything wrong, is it? So grandma could show me them. Unless she hasn't got any, that might explain it. I think I will ask her when we decide to tell her that we've been speaking to each other. I don't want to lose this yet either.

Your proposal to mum sounds so funny. If I ever propose to a girl I'll make sure I don't start it like that. You had to ask for permission? What are you, like two hundred years old? I'm amazed grandpa Norman didn't just laugh at you, or pretend to say no. That's what I'd do! He has been teaching me to play chess as well so if that ever happens to me it shouldn't take me four tries, and he certainly won't have to let me win. Not that I'll be asking anybody for permission anyway, ha ha! I have heard grandma talk about marriage and babies before to one of her friends, but I wasn't really listening. If she still thinks that it is wrong to have a baby before you are married then that is very old-fashioned. There is one girl who went to my primary school who was in the year above who is pregnant already. It was such a surprise when I saw it on Facebook, such a scary thought at this age. I didn't tell grandma, she doesn't really understand how it works with kids and that sort of thing today.

I did catch up with the football. I watched the Liverpool vs Chelsea game the other week, but I was really sorry that I did. It was really typical that it was Gerrard that slipped over, after everything you said about him. There's still a chance to win though, isn't there? Jack was trying to explain it to me the other day, if some teams lose and you win? Yeah Burnley are going up! I wish I had been able to go to some of the games, I messaged John about it on Facebook when I realised we had already been promoted and he said that he was at the game at the weekend, said it was like one big party, which I was a bit jealous about.

I didn't realise Samantha was a girl, sorry about that. It's good that you have stayed in touch even though you don't work together any more. If her dog is that stupid then it should be called Kevin, definitely. Grandpa Norman says dogs are like their owners, though, so maybe Samantha only called it Kevin because she is as stupid as the dog. Do you spend a lot of time with Samantha?

No no, school isn't rubbish because of them; I haven't played football this term yet so I haven't really seen them. It's rubbish because the teachers keep making us do GCSE work, you know, as like taster lessons. The way they go on about them you would think they are the ends of the world. Grandma and grandpa don't help either. They always try and get so involved with my schoolwork that I think they'll end up making my choices for me. There was one lesson in Science when that Josh Vickers boy was teasing the girl I was telling you about, the one who sits in front, about me. He was telling her that I was moving schools, which just isn't true, and she kept asking me about it. It was so stupid. It was him that told the music teacher that I was flirting with her as well, which was annoying, but never mind. Like Josh Vickers even knows what flirting is. I have said it before and I will say it again: nobody cares what he thinks.

Love,

Henry

Dear Henry,

I only called her Sam to be fair, so not your fault, fella. Could easily have been a boy or a girl! That's a bit mean about her and her dog though. I have heard that saying before like but it's definitely not true for Samantha. You shouldn't call people stupid. A bit disrespectful to be honest that, mate. I don't spend loads of time with her, no, the odd weekend here and there, walking the dog sometimes, just that sort of thing.

Really well done on getting moved up for Science. That's ace, mate, good work. I wouldn't worry about the hard work for the GCSEs that they're making you do now, they're probably just trying to scare you into working harder for them next year. Your nan and granddad just want what is best for you too, fella, so don't give them too much of a hard time. I know it's irritating with all the work and that, dealing with this Josh Vickers kid and everything, and I know you'll have heard this a thousand times before, but school is the easiest you'll get it, trust me, so try and enjoy it. It sounds like you have a bit of a laugh in Science with this girl anyway. What's her name? What's she like? If you want to chat to her at lunch times you know, you should just try and catch her before hand and ask if she wants to chill with you for a bit, or something, I dunno really. I wouldn't keep winding her up in lessons though, you don't want to get her into any serious trouble and for her to blame you, do you? Besides, if she finds it funny then, maybe, like, you two could be proper mates or something instead. Does she know your mate, Mollie? Maybe you could get Mollie to say something to her for you. I'm afraid I'm a bit like your nan and granddad on this stuff though, fella, I don't really understand how it works with you lot today either.

I can't say it's any real surprise that your nan hasn't shown you pictures of me, mate. She never really liked me to be honest, it was always your Norman who I got on better with, and we know who wears the pants in their relationship, like, so if she didn't want you to see them you wouldn't have.

We'll have less of this 200 years old malarkey, please! It wasn't that long ago that everybody had to ask the bride's dad's permission to marry her. It is silly though, I see what you mean. I think I did it more to help me win them over than for your mum's sake. As if your granddad has got you playing chess already as well. No I don't reckon it would take you four tries either, not with your brains, I bet you're already quality at it. It's not your nan's fault that she's old-fashioned, like. That was just the done thing when she was growing up. Her mum would have gone mad and probably disowned her if she had had your mum before she got married to your granddad, so it just sort of passes on like that. I can't believe you know somebody who is pregnant already, though, I definitely wouldn't tell your nan that. Some people your age are so desperate to grow up, it's not all good you know, fella. I know I sound like an old fart saying it, but sometimes it's best to just enjoy being a kid for now and worry about all of that when you get a bit older. It doesn't sound like we have to worry about you introducing any girls to your nan and granddad just yet though.

Ah mate, I'm sorry you watched that one. It was heart-breaking. I don't really want to talk about it to be honest, mate. Sorry. Great for Burnley though yeah, sounds like your mate John had a cracking time at the match, always great watching the celebrations when a team reaches the Prem. Bournemouth haven't done too badly either, amazing achievement to finish that highly in their first season. Last time I went the fans were buzzing.

Love,

Robert

Dear Robert,

I didn't mean to be nasty about Sam. It was just a phrase that I heard grandpa Norman say. I'm sure she's lovely. Besides, if you're just friends who walk the dog then you've nothing to worry about anyway, right? Even if it turns out she isn't as clever as mum was.

Thanks, I know my GCSEs are important and stuff, I just don't want to have to worry about them yet. I'm worried I might make the wrong choices and then end up hating the lessons I'm doing, but by then it'll be too late, won't it? I did what you said and I got to chat a bit more with Chloe, that's the girl's name, by the way. She wanted to know if I was really moving schools again, but I told her it was just Josh Vickers being stupid. It turns out he picks on her quite a lot in school. I thought I had it a bit rubbish because I don't really get to play football any more, but she has it really bad. Apparently there are other girls, ones in the year above, who ganged up on her after school once before Easter for texting a boy in their year, so she stopped. She didn't seem very bothered by it all, but I think secretly she is, I think she is a bit scared of them. She showed me some of the texts that the older girls have sent to her as well, and they're horrible. She just deletes them now but I think that's why she's been in the Quiet Study so much this term. She sits with Jack, Mollie and me at lunch and break times now though, so that's good at least. Plus it means I get to chat to her some more, which is fine by me.

Why didn't grandma Lynne like you? You are so right; she is definitely in charge. Everything in the house is always exactly where she wants it to be. It's so irritating that I can't ask her about you, with you being dead. Or fake-dead, you know? I don't really get how you would go about doing that, though. How did you do it? It's like something out of a ghost film, or a horror, don't you think? Sending letters to a man who is technically dead! Actually, I hope it is nothing like a horror, because that means it's got a bad ending. If you faked your own death though, didn't you have to change your name? When you moved to Bournemouth, I mean? If you were Robert Henderson when you lived in Liverpool, are you called something else now? Does Samantha call you Robert, or have you lied to her about it? Have you told her about me?

It's really weird that that was a thing when grandma was growing up. The 'no sex before marriage' rule, I mean. Do you think grandma Lynne is Catholic? If she came from a Catholic family? That would explain why grandma is so against it. It definitely doesn't apply so much nowadays, ha ha! See! That's exactly my point though, about school and everything. I just want to carry on being me and being young for a bit longer but school are all 'no you have to work hard and do your GCSEs and A Levels and go to uni and get a job and retire and die', and I'm thinking that all sounds like it'll take forever and be rubbish.

I am in no rush to bring anybody home to meet grandma and grandpa. Don't be absurd, Robert. That would mean having a proper girlfriend, and I cannot be bothered with that yet. I get enough drama from Jack constantly wanting to ask Molly out but never actually doing it, why on Earth would I want that for myself?

Sorry for bringing up the football. I saw that Liverpool didn't win the league, but second is still amazing!

Bournemouth have done really well, yeah, but not as well as Burnley, woo! Who do you think will win out of Burnley and Liverpool next year?

Love,

Henry

Dear Henry,

Your GCSEs are not the end of the world. You haven't even started them yet, you nutter, stop panicking over them. I'm glad you're mates with that Chloe girl, it sounds like she could use a mate who'll listen to her at the moment. If she is having a hard time of it you should really tell the teachers though, mate. Nothing will get solved if you just let it carry on. You should tell her she's doing the right thing in ignoring the texts though, best not to respond to stuff like that, I reckon. Kids can be cruel, but you just have to rise above it. Why don't you ask her if she fancies doing something at the weekend, or something? Might help take her mind off school for a bit, and who knows, you might stop flapping about these GCSEs you don't even do yet.

I've got a few ideas why she wouldn't like me, but it's a long story, mate. I'll explain it another time. I think she always thought your mum could do better, especially after having been to uni and that. I think she thought that once your mum moved away she'd grow out of being with me eventually, but she didn't. I've always wondered if there might be a part of her that blames me for her not being here any more as well. The important thing is it's nothing for you to worry about.

I know what you mean, fella, about me being technically dead. It's not ideal. I used to forget myself, like, when I was asked for my name and that on the phone, or when I was looking for work. Always had to think about it, which just makes you look stupid straightaway, like you can't remember your own name, or dead suspicious. I'll tell you how I did it properly when you're older, mate. But yeah I did have to change my name, and no, it's not Robert Henderson any more. But that's the name that I would have always used around you and that because technically you should be Henry Henderson, which I always thought sounded pretty cool, to be honest. Like a comic book character or something. I could always imagine Henry Henderson as like a Clark Kent or Bruce Wayne kind of name, I dunno why. Samantha doesn't know it's not my real name either. She calls me something else. Mate, I'm sorry, but, I can't really risk telling you what my other name is, not just yet anyway. Samantha knows that I've got a son by a previous marriage, and that I recently got back in touch with him after a few years of not being in contact. She doesn't really know any more than that.

Yeah that is a Catholic rule, and your nan is Catholic for sure, mate, I'm amazed you haven't noticed. She used to have all the usual crucifixes and that in the house when I went round. My mum was mad on it as well when we were growing up, but then you got that round Liverpool loads back then, my dad used to say it was because of the Irish influence. It definitely doesn't really apply as much these days, you're right, but you shouldn't be worrying about anything like that just yet. You just keep doing what you're doing, fella. Maybe you could introduce Chloe to your nan and granddad eventually though, ay? (wink wink)

Not really, mate. Nobody ever remembers who finished in second. If we weren't gonna win the league then I'd have rather we weren't in the running at all. Hurts getting that close, you know? I think if we can keep hold of Suarez then your Burnley team don't stand a chance though next year. Did you see what he did to Norwich?

Samantha is lovely, yeah. I know you didn't really mean to be mean about her, I probably took it the wrong way to be honest, fella. Was probably just me being a bit sensitive about it.

Love,

Robert

Dear Robert,

Yes, you're quite right. I shouldn't worry so much. You're right about Chloe too, I think it is helping her just having somebody to listen to her. I don't think she gets much chance to talk about it at home, so I suppose she needs to vent to somebody. I keep telling her that we have to do something about the texts and the bullying, but she says she'd rather just ignore it until they get bored and it goes away. I don't know how long that might take though, so I'm a bit worried for her. I am not introducing Chloe to grandma and grandpa. Not how you meant it anyway. She is not my girlfriend. I'll introduce her as a friend, maybe. Eventually. I have invited her out over the weekend though, like you said. I think we are going to get the bus into Blackburn to the shopping centre. Unless grandpa Norman wants to give us a lift, but then I would have to introduce Chloe to him, so I probably won't even ask him.

That's a bit cruel of grandma if it is true. It sounds to me like mum did well to find someone like you. Not many people would drive four hours to see the person they love. But then again, grandma can be very stubborn like that. I think maybe after mum died she stopped being a proper Catholic as well. She is still very strict sometimes, but all the crosses and stuff you mentioned have gone. How could she blame you for mum dying though? I thought you said mum died giving birth? That doesn't make it your fault.

I think I sort of understand why you can't tell me your new name. I do think I'm old enough now, to hear how you did it. Please tell me, it can be our little secret.

Does that mean that nobody will remember that Burnley finished second as well? That would be a shame; I thought they did really well to get promoted this season. If we still have Austin and Ings, though, Suarez might not be able to score more than they can! I will definitely be watching that game.

I don't suppose you ever found any pictures of you and mum under your bed that you could send over, did you? Send one of Samantha, too! I would like to see what she looks like; especially since you two are good friends. No, wait, I have an even better idea. Send me a picture of her dog! If I have any pictures of my friends and me then I will send them to you in return. When are you next seeing Samantha?

Love,

Henry

Dear Henry,

Right, mate, first things first, you never blame yourself for your mum. I know you didn't exactly, but I just want to put this to bed. She died of PPH. That's Postpartum haemorrhage, or Postpartum bleeding. All it means is that your mum was bleeding while she was giving birth to you, and that they couldn't stop it in time to save her. It had nothing to do with you, it just happens sometimes. It's actually dead rare to die from it in the UK nowadays, but that's just how these things go sometimes, mate. It had absolutely nothing to do with you. Don't ever blame yourself for it. Your mum would be heartbroken if she ever thought you felt like that. If you want someone to blame, fella, blame me. I was the one that couldn't look after you properly, I'm why you ended up with your nan and granddad in the first place. If I'd really been ready to have a kid, then I wouldn't have let you down so badly. Your mum would have never let you go. I just wanted to clear that up with you, you know, before anything else.

How was your weekend with Chloe? What did you do in the shopping centre? Hope you had a good time. Did you get a goodbye kiss? (only messing)

Ah no mate, it's totally different with the Championship I suppose. People will remember who finished second in that because you still get the automatic promotion with it, so like, it still comes with a prize really. Burnley have done really well, mate, you'll have to try and get to Turf Moor to watch them next season.

I finally found some pictures to send over! There's one

of me and your mum together at her graduation, turns out I did have them after all, they were in the bottom of the wardrobe. I've also put in one of me from last year when I ran the Bournemouth half-marathon. Ignore the stupid face I'm pulling, it was harder than I thought it would be. Never doing one of them again, nearly killed me all over again! Samantha said it would be a bit weird to send a picture of her in the same letter as one of your mum, so I haven't got one of her, but she did give me one of Kevin to send to you. That's him snoring in his bed, where he spends probably about 23 hours out of every day. I hope they get to you okay, and don't worry about sending any of them back, you're sound to keep those.

I saw Samantha over the weekend actually, we were meant to be taking Kevin out again but the weather was rubbish down here so we stayed in hers watching films and that instead. I'm taking her fishing next week if the weather picks up a bit. You wouldn't think it was Summer...

Love,

Robert

Dear Robert,

That sounds just awful. I'm so sorry I brought it up and made you talk about it again; it must be so sad for you. I know it must be because it was sad for me – I cried reading your last letter, and I never even knew her. Did she even get to see me? Properly I mean, before she died? I don't want to blame myself, but I definitely don't want to blame you for what happened either. I think you did what you thought was best. Also, you could have just left it alone and we might never have spoken to each other, but I think it was really brave of you to send me that first letter.

Shut up about Chloe! No I did not get a goodbye kiss! We had a good time; she's really quite funny once you get her talking. She has told her form teacher all about the texts now and she hasn't had one since because the girls all got suspended. She still gets shouted at when they see her, because now they're calling her a snitch and stuff, but she says if she stays away from them then it doesn't make any difference. Josh Vickers still winds her up in Science, but that's just him being stupid, and he does that to loads of people, so nobody really cares. We went into Sports Direct to look at the football shirts while we were in Blackburn and she accidentally knocked over one of the tennis ball buckets. I say 'accidentally', but I think she did it on purpose to make me laugh. I used to think she was such a swot, but she is actually quite naughty sometimes. She felt really bad about it though, and we ended up spending like fifteen minutes helping the shop people to collect them all up. It was so funny though, she went, like, bright pink, she was so embarrassed! I actually mentioned to Chloe that I wanted to go to Turf Moor to watch the Burnley Liverpool game next season, and she said that she would love to come with me if we can go. She has never been to a football match before, but she said it sounds really exciting. After we had been to the shopping centre we got the bus back to her house, because she said that her mum wasn't going to be in for ages and her TV is great for just chilling and watching films on and stuff. I stayed there until way after it had gone dark, and then I had to call grandpa for a lift home. He wasn't too happy that I had gone back to Chloe's without telling him that's what I was doing, but he didn't tell grandma so it was fine in the end.

Thank you thank you thank you for the pictures! The one of you and mum is amazing. She looked so pretty and clever in her robes, even if she is wearing one of those stupid hats that look like placemats, and you looked really smart in your suit! Samantha's dog is very cute, but I can see what you mean about him, he looks like a bit of a dopey dog. He is really big, much bigger than I had imagined him. I have had a look for some to send over to you, but I can't find any good ones at the moment. I will keep looking and send them soon. What did Samantha mean by it would be weird sending one with mum? I don't understand. She didn't even know mum, did she?

It's really cool that you ran a half-marathon, I was going to ask you where you finished and stuff, but, I already know. Look, Robert, I don't want to lie to you and pretend that I didn't, but I searched for the picture that you sent me on the Bournemouth running results page-thing. It took a while to find the right picture but I did in the end. You finished 206th, right? That's really good considering how many people were running and how hard you said it was! I think you were just being modest really; you could run another one easily. I also found out what your real name is. Well, not your real name, obviously, but the name that you are using now (because your real 'real' name is Robert, right?) You were runner number 12831, and your name now is James Rayner. I'm really sorry if you didn't want me to know about that, but you mentioned the half-marathon and I had the pictures and it was just too tempting. I won't tell anybody, and I will keep calling you Robert, if you like? Your secret is safe with me, don't worry. I hope you aren't angry with me.

Love,

Henry

Dear Henry,

That's okay, fella, it's normal for you to have questions about your mum, fire away, I don't mind. She didn't get to see you, mate, no. Sorry. She was unconscious before you were delivered and then once you were born they whisked her away and that was that. She turned to me while she was in labour to say that she was feeling faint and didn't think she could keep pushing, that's when they first thought there might be a problem. I made a joke about how it wasn't too late, if she was feeling that bad they can put it back and wait until another day. She just laughed dead breathily, and told me I was an idiot. That was the last thing I ever heard her say. I watched them roll her out of that delivery room, through those big swinging double doors, and I just thought everything was fine, you know? It was about half an hour later they called me into a little side room. When they do that you know straight away it's bad news, mate. I thought they were gonna tell me that we'd lost you during the birth, it'd never even crossed my mind that I might lose her. It didn't hit me properly for weeks. I kept calling for her, the first few days, like she was in the next room. Or expecting the phone to ring to ask for a lift. When we got you home and she just wasn't there, but her stuff was still all over the place. Her breakfast from the day we left for the hospital still half eaten on the table. I was in the van on the M6 when it set in. It was like someone pushed a button, and everything inside of me just fell out. I was just empty. You were crying because of the noise of the van and I was trying to see to you while steering through the traffic on my way to a job I was already late for, and I just cried. I'm glad you were okay with me getting in touch after so long.

You're good on those computers aren't you? I should have known that picture was online and that there was a chance you might find it. Not much point in hiding it now. That's my new name yeah, James Rayner. That's what I get called in work, that's what Sam calls me and all. I didn't really choose it in the sense that I got to pick a name for myself, I knew if I did that I'd end up going for something dead stupid, something like Max Power, dead obvious, you know? I remembered seeing a van in Reading when your mum lived down there, a plumbing company I think that was based somewhere around there. It came to me dead randomly one day, the memory of it, and I just thought it was a good, plain name to help me blend in and that. It took a bit of getting used to like, but I expected that. I'm not angry with you for finding it out, I would have only had to tell you eventually anyway. I would have preferred to do it in my own time like, but never mind. That's what I get for having a smart kid. Suppose I can blame your mum for that. My real name is Robert though, same name I had back when I was living in Liverpool. I know I can count on you to keep it all to yourself. I might get onto the marathon picture in work actually, see if I can get it taken down before anyone else recognises me.

I was only winding you up about Chloe. She sounds like a really nice girl, doesn't sound like she deserves the grief that the older kids keep giving her. I told you though, soon as you tell someone these things can be sorted out. Made up she did and that it's getting better. Ignore that Josh kid though, he sounds like a meff anyway. I reckon

Chloe might have a bit of a thing for you, mate. Call it my instincts or whatever, but I reckon that while you're all about being 'mates' with her she might have her eye on something a bit more than that. Careful! Don't go being reckless with her feelings, either, if you really aren't interested.

No worries on the pictures, fella, thought it'd be good for you to see what your arl fella looked like. Don't let your nan and granddad find them, though, or they'll start wondering where they came from. Would be great to see some pictures of you, like, if you've found them yet. I haven't seen you since you were a baby, would be good to see if you ended up with my ears or if you dodged that bullet. Kevin is massive, isn't he? Yeah he's a properly dumb dog, his tail is still going like a whirlwind as well, he knocked a cup of scolding hot tea all over Sam's new jeans the other day, should have heard the noise she made. Shouldn't have been funny, but it was a bit.

Sam didn't want to send one because she thought it might be weird you seeing her in the same set as your mum. She doesn't want you to feel like she might be replacing her or anything, you know, because obviously she's not. We're going away together over the weekend, just down the coast to Brighton where her parents live. Gonna get some fishing done down there and all, if I have anything to say about it! Did you ever ask Norm about taking you out round yours?

Love,

Robert

Dear Robert,

I'm afraid I don't understand, Robert. How can she be worried about sending over a picture and replacing mum if you are just friends? She could never replace mum, obviously. Surely she knows that.

That is a shame about mum. It sounds like she deserved much better than that. At least I get to see her now, even if it is only in the pictures around the house and the ones you sent me.

I still don't have any good pictures of my friends or myself, so I can't send them over yet. Also I don't think you're right about Chloe. She's really nice, but she is quite ugly. I get the impression that she'd rather be by herself at the moment than have a boyfriend. So that's fine. I will just stay as her friend whenever she needs me; I think that's better anyway.

I hope you have fun in Brighton.

From,

Henry

Dear Henry,

Sorry I didn't get back to you sooner, I think I might have upset you a bit with my last letter, so I wanted to give you a bit of time to calm down and that. I should have explained it earlier to you, mate, but I was worried you might take it badly. Sam and I are together now. Well, I think we've been together a while to be honest but like I said, I didn't want to make things awkward for you or anything. I didn't want to tell you until I'd had a chance to chat to her about it a bit, see if she was all right with me spreading the news to you and that. I couldn't be happier with her, if I'm honest, mate. She's great, she really is. I hope you aren't too annoyed that I didn't tell you earlier. If you ever get the chance to meet her I think you would get on dead well with her. She's keen to meet you one day as well, mate. But obviously that'll be up to you, if and when it happens.

What's Chloe done to do your head in now, like? Bit harsh calling her ugly, isn't it? I'm sure that's not the case, mate, and even so, it's not about what people look like, it's about what they're like and how well you get along with them. That's why Sam and I stayed so close after she left our office. I reckon that's why you get along so well with this Chloe girl, and why you're so irritated by whatever it is she's done. You've already said she's dead funny and that you like her, and it sounds like you've helped her with a lot of personal stuff and that, so don't let whatever has happened get to you or change what you really think of her. You know what I mean? You have to give people a chance sometimes, fella. Don't go being wicked to her face either, you might end up regretting it when she wants nothing to do with you.

Obviously Samantha will never replace your mum, mate. Nobody ever could, but I can't live forever by myself feeling sorry about what happened, can I? That's just daft.

I hope you're all right, mate.

Love,

Robert

Dear Robert,

I think it's great, good for you. I'm really happy for you both. I'm not angry. It would have been nice to hear about it a bit sooner, but that's fine.

Chloe is fine. She hasn't done anything. We get on well because she is a good friend and tells me things when they happen.

You're right. Nobody will ever replace mum.

From,

Henry

Dear Robert,

I haven't heard from you for a few weeks, so I thought I would write again, just to check that you got my last letter, and that everything is okay. I'm really sorry about what I said last time. I was very short with you and I had no reason to be, really. I wasn't sure how to take the news that you and Samantha were together. I suppose with having just heard all of your memories of mum it still feels very recent to me. I didn't really think at the time that it must be like ancient history for you by now. You're right, I think, you do need to move on eventually. I just didn't know what to say. Samantha sounds lovely and I would love to meet her one day, obviously not before I have met you. I don't think we would be able to see each other over Christmas though because grandma Lynne says it is always a very hectic time of year and that wouldn't be much good for anybody. But soon, maybe. How was your trip to Brighton with Samantha? How is Kevin? I hope he is still just as dopey and his tail is still spilling tea everywhere, but I hope Samantha's leg is okay.

I'm sorry I was short about Chloe as well. She had started texting that boy from the year above again and I didn't know why because he is a weirdo and he is really mean to her most of the time. I tried to ask her what it is she likes about him but she doesn't like to talk to me about it. She just goes quiet and tries to change the subject. It is so annoying. I only called her ugly because I was frustrated with her. She calls herself ugly though so I guess it's fine really. She says that she is really spotty and that she will never get married because nobody will ever think she is pretty enough. I want to tell her that that's rubbish, I have once or twice, but she doesn't really listen. And now she is texting that other boy again. I don't even know his name, I don't know anything about him really, but I know that he upsets Chloe because I have seen her crying in school twice, even though she tries her hardest to hide it. I don't really know what I can do. She is struggling with some of her teachers as well. I think she gets stuck quite often with her schoolwork, but her mum isn't in the house a lot of the time so she doesn't really have anybody to ask for help. I keep telling her that Jack, Molly and I can help her with it but she doesn't listen to that either. She has never told the teachers that she needs some extra tuition or anything, so they just shout at her for not doing her assignments and stuff. It's not good for her, especially now that we've started on the GCSE work and the coursework all matters towards our grades and stuff. I finally decided on my GCSE subjects, by the way. In the end grandma and grandpa let me choose for myself, which was a pleasant surprise. I am doing Spanish, which I am really glad about, or 'made up' with, as you might say - ha ha. I decided to do History instead of Geography because even though History with Mr Derbyshire was boring it was still better than Geography. I am rubbish at Geography. I have to do Maths, Science and English because the school says they are compulsory subjects, which is rubbish because I didn't really want to keep doing English because of the people in my class. Josh Vickers is in it, as well as some of the boys that call Jack a crow. One of them who I really don't like has had to repeat the year, which is just typical. I think you'll really like one of my choices... I decided to do drama! Chloe was doing it and it was either that or Religious Studies, and I really wasn't interested much in that, plus it's all the way on the top floor so it is such an effort to get to every lesson, so I thought why not? It's the only lesson that I will be doing with Chloe so that was another good reason. I thought that you could help me out with things if I get stuck, maybe? Because you've done it before. I asked Chloe and she said that for our exams we have to do a scripted piece in our first year and then we have to make up our own for our second year. The first one should be okay; if you have any ideas of good plays then let me know! I'm not looking forward to the second performance though. I wouldn't even know where to start when it comes to writing a play. Then again, hopefully I will be in the same group as Chloe so maybe she will know what to do. I think year ten is much harder than years seven, eight and nine combined, and we are only in the first month or so! The teachers treat us like the older students now though, so I suppose that it's better in that sense.

I thought you might like to know that grandma Lynne spoke to me a little about you over the Summer. I didn't tell her how much I knew about you, of course, but she brought it up one day when we were talking about mum. I really don't think that she hates you as much as you think she does. I didn't get that impression anyway. I never got around to asking grandpa Norman if we could go fishing, but I did try and do some by myself. It was a disaster. I had a look in the shed and asked grandpa if we had any old fishing rods lying around. I managed to find something that I thought I could use, so I took it down to the stream with Chloe, Jack and Mollie. We bought a tin of sweetcorn on the way, because I didn't really know what to use as bait and Jack said that he had seen it on a fishing programme once. It was only when we got there that I realised I had forgotten to look for a hook for the end of the string, so I spent ages tying it around the sweetcorn instead. Mollie was laughing so much because it just kept slipping out of the loop I made and into the stream. There was sweetcorn everywhere. When we finally put it in the water it didn't even sink, it just sort of sat on the top of the water and drifted in the current a bit. It was really funny just watching this lonely piece of sweetcorn that was all tied up just bobbing about. We didn't try it for long because we realised it definitely wasn't going to work, plus it was a really sunny day so it was more fun to paddle in the stream anyway. I don't even know if there are any fish in there, but I think I probably would have had a better chance at catching them if I had used my bare hands.

What do you think of the new football season? I thought it started so early this year but Jack said that it usually starts mid-August. How do you think Liverpool are doing? They seem to be struggling a lot more now that Suarez has gone, were you happy to see him leave after he bit that man in the World Cup? Burnley are having a terrible season; they haven't won a game yet. The Liverpool versus Burnley match won't be worth watching if they carry on like this. Jack keeps teasing me and saying that they will definitely get relegated this season, but I think once we win a couple we should be okay. I've just had a look online, and the first Burnley versus Liverpool match is on Boxing Day! At first I thought that was terrible because it means I wouldn't be able to go, but I think I will ask grandma and grandpa for tickets to the match for Christmas, then I will definitely get to go! How are Bournemouth doing so far?

Again, Robert, I am so sorry for how short I was with you in my last letter. I hope you don't hate me now, and that we can carry on sending letters to each other, because I feel like I was really getting to know you and that we were getting very close. I would love that to carry on.

Love,

Henry

Dear Henry,

I'm really sorry I didn't send you much in the way of letters over the summer, mate. It was really good to hear from you though. I'll do my best not to let it take so long again. Don't worry about the thing with Sam, I dunno how I expected you to take it, to be honest. I know it's a lot to get your head around. I get that all the stuff I'm telling you about your mum must feel dead new and that, makes sense, like. It doesn't feel like ancient history to me, but obviously I've lived through it before and it was a long time ago now, so it isn't always on my mind any more. I can understand it being a bit weird when your dad gets with someone new, that was bound to happen, fella. Just give it a chance. As you say, we haven't even met each other yet, so there's nothing to worry about anyway. I think your nan is probably right about it being a bad time in the run up to Christmas, but maybe the New Year would be a better time to arrange something? Our trip to Brighton was good fun cheers, we actually went back down there for a couple of weeks over the summer. We took Kevin with us so he could cover Sam's parent's carpet in coffee for once instead. He's still as dopey as ever, but Sam's leg is sound now. It was good to just get away for a bit, away from work and all of that. Always great to spend some time just me and Sam as well, you know? We got to talk about a few things that we had been putting off for a bit, so it was well worth going. Still didn't get to do any fishing though.

What are you like? Sounds like you had a good laugh with your mates, like, but you're mad trying to fish without the proper gear. You need weights, mate, that's what makes the bait sink. Even if they're just the little ones. You definitely need a hook as well. Think about it, if a fish bites on the end of your tied up sweetcorn how are you gonna pull it out of the water, you barmpot? You probably would have had more luck doing it with your bare hands, you're not wrong. Sweetcorn actually wasn't a bad shout from Jack, you can use it as bait, but again, fella, you'd be better off getting some proper bait if you're gonna be fishing a stream. Another thing I thought of when I read your letter was if it was shallow enough to paddle in, what made you think there was gonna be any fish in there? Didn't half make me laugh reading about it though. Funny that, mate. You definitely get your fishing skills from your granddad, by the sounds of it. Next time you fancy it you should just ask him, he'd love to go with you I'm sure.

Football hasn't been good enough so far. Neither Burnley nor Liverpool are having much joy at the moment, are they? I was devastated when we let Suarez go, I thought we had at least one more season of him at least, and I dunno what we were thinking, trying to replace him with that Balotelli, he's done nothing so far. Lazy sod. Going to see the Burnley Liverpool game would be a good laugh, maybe you should get in touch with your old mate, John, and ask him if he fancies it as well. He could go with you instead if your granddad wasn't interested. I know how little football he used to watch. Good idea getting them as Christmas presents as well, gives you something to look forward to, like. I love the Boxing Day games, wouldn't be Christmas without them. Bournemouth aren't doing too badly. Mixed bag of results so far, but then it's still early days yet, and it is the Championship, so you never know what's gonna happen.

Wasn't sure what to make of you talking to your nanny Lynne about me, like. Good to hear that you don't reckon she hates me, and I suppose it's nice that she's finally prepared to talk about me, but I'm not so sure. Was a relief to hear that they didn't force any GCSE choices on you in the end. Some sound choices in there and all. Spanish was a given after how much you said you enjoy it. I reckon you'll do dead well in that one. Teachers will start giving you more respect, yeah, you're getting to be some of the oldest in the school now, it's that time when they start expecting you to act like it. Unlucky! English is still important, mate. Don't let the divvies in your class put you off it too much. Just think, the better at English you get, the better your letters are gonna sound, and the smarter I'm gonna think you are. Drama is a mad choice though. I was made up you thought of me, like, but you should have picked something that you were interested in. Drama isn't really something I can help you with in letters either, mate. I will wherever I can, like, of course I will, but I mean there's not much I can say about how to perform when this is all words on a page, is there? Maybe once we've met a few times I'll be able to help you out a bit more with it. It does make sense that you'd want a class with Chloe though.

Actually, mate, I wanted to talk to you about this Chloe thing. I dunno how things are now, like, between the two of you, and if she is still texting that lad from the year above, but you shouldn't let that bother you too much. She'll figure out for herself if he's bad news, you have to let her make her own mistakes. That's what mates are for, to be there to pick up the pieces. By the sounds of it she would be better off without him, like, but she has to realise that for herself, mate. All I'll say is think about it. If she is still spending loads of time with you and that, then how interested in this other fella is she, really? She shouldn't be calling herself ugly either. You should tell her that being really beautiful isn't about how you look, it's about who you are. Or tell her something like that anyway. Don't use what I said, because it sounds rubbish now I've read it back. Besides, all these pictures of the celebs you see in magazines and that are all fake anyway. Trust me, Sam can do it on the computer, she works in that side of things now and all, doing adverts for the magazines and that. Maybe you and Chloe could do some coursework together if she has trouble doing it at home? If she doesn't seem keen on the idea then just work it into conversation and that. Sit with her while you both work on it or something, or get Jack and Mollie and that to all sit together and do it at a lunchtime when you're altogether. You'll either get loads done or you'll just end up messing about and having a laugh, but either way it'll be more fun than struggling through it on your own, like. Either way it sounds like she's having a bit of a hard time at the moment and all you can do is be there for her, my mate. Just make sure that no matter how upset she gets you stay happy and try to keep making her laugh. And just listen to her. In the end she'll feel better and she'll appreciate you being there for her. Trust me, it's how me and Sam ended up together. Not that I'm suggesting you and Chloe should end up together, or that you want to, or that you want a proper girlfriend yet or anything, it was just an example. Don't go kicking off again. I'm only messing with you.

Write back soon, fella, let's not leave it as long this time.

Love,

Robert

Dear Robert,

Don't worry about the lack of letters; it was as much my fault as it was yours. The important thing is that we are back in touch now. I am sure that Samantha and you will be very happy together. I quite like the idea of meeting up in the New Year, we will have to see if we can find a good time for it. I was thinking though, it is unlikely that I will be able to travel anywhere to meet you by myself, so I would have to tell grandma or grandpa about it, which means telling them the extent to which we've been in touch over the past year. I'm not sure how they would react to that, so I think for now maybe it is better to take it slowly and I will fill them in gradually over the coming months. I have already started, I suppose, since I mentioned you to grandma Lynne over the Summer. I will see if I can bring you up again and, eventually, if she asks me about it, I will tell her that you have been in touch. Then she should feel better about me meeting you, at least. Did I tell you what she did when I mentioned you? She went and found my birth certificate. I don't know if you remember mentioning it, but it did say you were an electrician after all!

I know, the fishing trip was a silly idea really, but it was more just to get my friends and I out for the day and near to the water. Ever since we took our trip to Ireland and I have read about your love for the coast I have wanted to spend as much time as I could near water. I started trying to drink lots more of it at first, but that didn't really do anything. Actually, it did make my skin feel amazing, so soft and smooth, so that was good. When I found the stream that runs past the community centre I decided that I would take a day and just follow it. It goes right behind my old primary school, I had no idea! I followed it and eventually it just sort of stops as it goes underground, at least I think that's where it went. It gets so shallow that you can walk in it and it barely touches your ankles, then it gets so narrow you can barely see where it actually is any more. It's amazing to think that if I followed it the other way, and kept going, and kept going and going, that eventually it would get really deep and I would have to swim. If I could swim for long enough, or if I got out and I walked along the bank instead, grandpa Norman says that it would take me all through Lancashire and towards Liverpool! He says that the water that flows through that tiny brook at the back of my primary school is the same water that eventually flows underneath the Liver Buildings and into the River Mersey, then into the Irish Sea. How amazing is that? To think, you have more than likely watched the water that is near the Liver Building, and that water could have come from right next to where I live. That's amazing, when you think about it. I bet if I followed it further along there are plenty of fish in it too. I mean, you're right, it would definitely help if I had all of the right equipment first, but I bet I could catch something if I had all of that and I went a bit further along it. I bet even grandpa Norman could catch something. Is that where you and him used to fish? We could have even fished in the same water; wouldn't that be crazy?

No, you're quite right, the football has been rubbish for both of us so far. Like you said though, it is a long season and there are still plenty of games left to play. It could get a lot better for us both yet. I mentioned getting some Burnley tickets to grandpa. As you guessed, he wasn't particularly interested in going to the football, but he did say that if I really wanted to go and there was nobody else I could go with then he would take me, which is great news for when I ask for the Burnley versus Liverpool tickets.

Ugh don't talk about me being the oldest in the school, it is so frustrating. I swear that the teachers think that now we're a Summer holiday older they can just expect that we're adults all of a sudden. Miss Wormald asked me to monitor the queues at lunchtime the other day, just to make sure that the year seven and eight kids weren't fighting. It was on my lunch break as well, like after six weeks off I all of a sudden don't get hungry anymore! The year sevens are all so small and annoying, and their blazers are far too big for them. It is like their parents have bought one in the hope that it will last them for the whole time they have to wear it. There's this one little blonde boy who looks so small in his that he looks more like a coat hanger with legs than he does an actual real life person.

I see what you mean about not being able to help me with drama through letters, the performances at least. I was talking more about the theory side of it, Chloe says that there are a lot of essays that we have to write, so I thought maybe if you had done that bit then you could help me out with those? It doesn't matter if you can't, I've been enjoying it anyway. I'm trying to convince Chloe to do the school play with me. I think she wants to really; she's just scared of being around some of the others who are in it who she doesn't get on with. I don't want to do it by myself though, so I haven't put my name down yet.

I think I get what you mean about the Chloe thing. I told her what you said, about pretty people not really being pretty if they aren't nice people. She didn't understand at first, but I spoke to her about it and told her that a 'friend of the family' works in adverts and explained what you said, about how all of those gorgeous celebrity pictures are faked on computers, which Chloe said she had heard of before but was never sure if it was true or not. She asked me if it's the same with the pictures you see on Facebook and Twitter and stuff? I have no idea about that, so I said I would ask my 'friend'. She isn't texting that boy in the year above now either, though I don't know how long that will last for. She says that she has had enough of him messing her about but we will see. He asked her out a couple of weeks ago and she was thinking about it for a while, but then while she was still thinking about it he asked somebody else out, so I think that showed her what he is really like. We had actually already done some coursework as a group before you suggested it! We all have the same History coursework, so we thought it would be good to try and do some of it together so we know that we have got at least some of it right. It's really helpful because Mollie is really good at History so we basically just copy everything off her. It definitely helped Chloe out.

What did you mean about it's how you and Samantha ended up together? Like you just kept making her laugh and eventually she wanted to go out with you?

Love,

Henry

Dear Henry,

I hadn't really thought about that. I dunno how keen your nan and granddad would be to see me after all this time and after everything that happened, especially back from the dead and that, so maybe break them in gently. They're gonna have to learn to live with it though, because I want to see you. I can't believe she pulled out your birth certificate, I knew it would say that. Was an all right job that, I miss it sometimes, was dead easy. Didn't take too much training either, I learned it all from my uncle Alan. If you don't end up going to uni or being a fire-fighter just give me a shout and we'll get you trained up in no time!

Made your skin feel soft? What are you on about? You come out with some mad things sometimes, you. You know I'd never even thought about that water thing you mentioned. I knew the Mersey could be tracked all the way into Wales somewhere but I'd never really thought about all the little rivers that must go up through Lancashire and that if you track it that way. Makes sense really I suppose with the amount of canals in Manchester. Crazy that the one at the back of your house leads all the way to the Liver Building, of course I've seen it! I used to walk past it all the time, it's right next to the waterfront and the docks and that, where your mum's favourite restaurants where. There are plenty of fish at our end, maybe you should follow it a bit if you decide to go again, definitely have more chance at catching something than in the 2-3 inches it sounds like you're on about. It's not miles away from where me and your granddad used to fish, no. We always went a bit further down, quieter spots away from the tourists and the drinkers on their nights out and that, especially if you went as far as like Otterspool prom. We'd usually go over the other side of the water as well, fish near New Brighton or Egremont, where the ferry is. I think your granddad only ever wanted to go down there because of the view of Liverpool though, to be honest. Was always a bit of a drive for him to get from yours all the way here just to do a bit of fishing, but then from the way you've described the waters round yours it sounds like he didn't have much choice.

Ay, you were there once as well, don't forget. With your blazer hanging over the ends of your wrists and your shiny new shoes and that. We've all been there, mate, don't go picking on the year 7s because they haven't scuffed up their school shoes yet. You of all people should know better than to make fun of anyone in school. Speaking of which, how did Chloe get on after all those texts and that? Has it calmed down now you're all a bit older? Sometimes you find that people just need a chance to grow up and mature a bit. Not you, like, the people who were sending them to her. Was good to hear she's come to her senses about that lad you don't like, even if it is only for now. If you like her then maybe now is the time for you to say something to her. I know you're gonna tell me that you don't, but it's dead obvious mate and I'm not gonna pretend that it isn't any more. You've gotta just be honest with her, maybe do what you did last time and ask her to go shopping with you or something. Buy her a Subway or whatever it is you lot get up to these days, and I'm sure she'll be more inclined to listen to what you've got to say. Let's be honest, from what I've heard you've been getting closer and closer, so isn't it about time you did something about it? While we're on the subject, actually, that is sort of what I meant, yeah. I just kept Sam happy, you know, when she got let go from work and that. I just sort of kept spending time with her, kept her spirits up. Laughing brings people together, mate, and I swear you'll know whether you really like someone when you see how they smile at you. Not like the smile they give teachers or when they're being polite and that, a proper smile. You'll know it when you see it. When it's just you and them and you've made her laugh and she'll look right at you, almost like she's not really looking at you, but like she can see inside your head. Then you'll know what I mean. Give it a go if you still aren't sure. Go 'ed lad, be brave! I'm glad you talked to her about it, you can tell her that all the Twitter and Facebook pictures are the same, yeah, I've literally just asked Sam while I was typing this for you. There you go, straight from the horse's mouth. There's nothing to be got from aspiring to be like the pictures in magazines, it's all a load of rubbish.

Do the school play. It'll be a right laugh, what is it they're doing? I reckon you'll enjoy it, I used to love the school plays. We did Sweeney Todd once in our school, was dead good that one. The one about the barber who cuts people's throats and then turns them into pies, you heard of it? It's dead gory, we had loads of blood packs squirting jets of blood on the audience and everything, was good fun.

Right, is there anything you want for Christmas that I can realistically send in the post? You know, without making your nan and granddad suspicious, like. If there is just let me know and I'll see what I can do to get it to you. I'd love to say that I thought of doing this all by myself, but Sam just came in with a cup of tea and asked me what I was getting you, so you can thank her.

Love,
Dad

Dear Dad,

I think grandma and grandpa would be thrilled to see you. I'm sure it would come as quite a shock to them to hear that you are still alive, of course, but that is something they are going to have to come to terms with eventually. I hate to break it to you though, dad, I don't want to be an electrician.

You don't have to get me anything for Christmas, it was really sweet of Samantha to suggest it, but you don't have to send me anything. I am quite happy to just keep in contact with you. Is it weird that I have started calling you dad, by the way? If it is then please just say the word and I will stop and go back to calling you Robert. It was weird when I first wrote it, I have to say, so I don't mind if you feel the same. I thought it would be better to ask than just to carry on one way or the other and let it be like an elephant in the room. Or in the letter, maybe, but that doesn't make any sense.

Chloe seems to be doing much better now. The texts have stopped and now that we help each other with coursework her grades have levelled out a bit. The teachers have stopped shouting at her, so that's something at least. She was 'made up' (as you would say - ha ha) to hear that Samantha said all of the celeb pictures are airbrushed and such, she said that it's a relief to know that she isn't broken if she's not perfect. I told her that she seemed pretty perfect to me. I was actually only making a joke to make her feel better (like you said), but she took it really seriously and I think that she thinks we're pretty much together. I haven't got a clue what you mean about all that smiling business, so I can't really say for sure if we are or we aren't. I should probably just ask her; it would be much easier. I know you will tell me to just go for it, but then it's easy for you, you don't actually have to see her!

I have signed up for the school play though. I even managed to convince Mollie and Chloe to do it with me. I tried to get Jack to do it as well but he just laughed about it, drama really isn't his thing. Sweeney Todd sounds awful, I'm glad we aren't doing that. We're doing A Midsummer Night's Dream. You know, the Shakespeare one? It is so hard to speak the lines though. Chloe says it gets easier the more you do it, but I'm not convinced. Why couldn't he just write it in normal English? I think we're performing it in February – next term, so I still have plenty of time to get to grips with it, I suppose. I would invite you to come and see it, but it is a long way for you to come for a school play and I don't think you would want to risk being back up this close to Liverpool. Maybe you can come to the next one. Unless it's Sweeney Todd, then I won't be in it.

So, every time I have ever asked you about it you have ignored it and moved onto something else, but you mentioned the whole 'being back from the dead' thing again in your last letter. I remember you saying that you would tell me once you thought I was old enough, well I think I am now, so how exactly did you fake your death? You can tell me and you know I will keep it a secret. I have kept everything else about you a secret so far, and it has just been eating away at me for a while. Did you plan it all out or did it just sort of happen and you thought you were really lucky? Or unlucky, I guess it depends on how you look at it.

Thank Samantha again for suggesting you get me a

Christmas present. It really was very nice of her.

Love,

Henry

P.S: There is nothing wrong with having smooth skin. Don't you mock me.

Dear Henry,

Obviously you don't want to be an electrician. I don't want you to be an electrician! I was only messing with you.

Of course you can call me dad. It does sound weird, you're right. It looks weird after all this time, but Henry, mate, it's all I've ever wanted, for you to call me dad. No that's a lie, actually. I wanted to earn it. 'Dad' isn't something that you just walk into being, it's something that you earn by raising your kid to be a good person. Anyone can have a baby and be a father, but you have to work at being a dad. My dad always said to me that if he raised me to be a better person than he was, then he had done his job in life. It's the same with me. I might have started the job a lot later than I wanted to, like, but then I'm usually late to everything anyway. It still applies though. I want to be involved in your life now and I want to see that I can do my job before it's too late. If I'm dead honest with you, I don't think I've earned the right to be called 'dad' yet, but if you think I have, or if you want to keep calling me it, then I'm never gonna argue with you, mate.

Anyway, that's all getting a bit heavy. I told Samantha what you said about not wanting anything off us for Christmas and she was having none of it, fella. She went out and got you a card and that anyway, and she's put a £20 iTunes voucher in it for you as well. I'm rubbish with this sort of thing, but it was her idea mate and she's insisted that I sent it with this letter, so enjoy! She says you can load up your jarg iPad with some music now! So Merry Christmas, mate! I hope you have a good one. If you check the envelope there's something else in there as well for you.

It's a present from me, so you don't have to ask your nan and granddad for them. Enjoy the match on Boxing Day, take your mate John or something if he wants to go.

I've actually got a bit of news about Sam and me, mate. I wasn't sure when or how to tell you because last time I mentioned her it didn't exactly go down dead well, but I wanna be completely honest with you. She's moved in with me, mate. Well, not quite. She hasn't moved in with me, because my place was tiny. We've both moved out of where we were and into a new flat together. And Kevin, of course. I wanted to tell you as soon as possible. It's also why my letters have been a bit few and far between lately, they probably will be for a bit yet, until we've swapped everything over to the new address, because I have to keep going back to the old flat to pick up your letters. I'll give you the new address once everything has settled down a bit. I hope you're all right with it and that. I knew you'd want me to tell you, even if you might not like it.

I was made up to hear about you and Chloe, I really was. I reckon you two are together now, it definitely sounds like it. If you aren't completely sure then I'd just ask her outright, it doesn't sound like you've got anything to worry about now. You two are good mates, it's only natural sometimes that you end up together. The beauty of getting with your mates is that when it goes well it makes for the best of relationships. You can trust me on that one, fella, I was with your mum. You'll know exactly what I'm on about with the smile when you see it. Quality that you'll be doing the play together as well. I never did a Shakespeare one believe it or not, for that very reason, mate. I could never get my head around the lines in them, but then I'm thick and never listened in school, and you're dead clever so keep at it, you've got ages, I'm sure you'll be sound with it. I would love to come and see the play, my mate, of course I would. You're right though, it is a bit dodgy for me to come all that way again. I'll save it for when we meet up first, which should be as soon as possible, yeah?

Of course there's nothing wrong with having smooth skin, but you're a lad, you can't just say stuff like that, it sounds mad!

Love,

Robert (Dad)

Dear Dad,

I have made my mind up, and I want to keep calling you that. You can keep trying to earn it, but while you're trying I still want to call you it.

Please tell Samantha thank you so much for the iTunes voucher, it's so generous of her. Tell her I am so grateful but that I haven't bought any music yet because I have no idea where to start. I have written a list of all the stuff I might possibly want to buy, and I will start narrowing it down from there. I will let her know what I decide upon. I can't believe you sent me the tickets, too. That was too much, you really didn't have to do that. I asked John if he would like to go to the match with me, but he said he already had a ticket so in the end Jack came with me. It was amazing. Well, it wasn't really, because we lost, but I had a good time regardless. I had a massive hot dog and bought a scarf that was half Liverpool and half Burnley, so that I had a souvenir of the game. Jack bought a pin badge even though he is a Manchester United fan. We were sat on one of the side bits, sort of close to the Liverpool fans. They were so noisy. There was a lot of shouting and then the two crowds started having an argument with each other through different songs. It was very funny but there was so much swearing. A big fat man sat next to us didn't stop swearing about the Liverpool players the whole time. I really wanted Burnley to score just so I could see what it's like when everybody celebrates. I saw the Liverpool fans doing it and it made me quite jealous. I think the match itself was probably a little bit boring, but I loved it. Thank you so much. I hope you two had an amazing Christmas together, I hope Santa brought you everything you asked for, ha ha!

That is such good news about you two moving in together. I understand why you were a little worried about telling me, after how I reacted last time, but it's fine, I am over it now. Besides, Samantha seems amazing (she sent me an iTunes gift-card, I mean, come on), so I think it's great that you two have settled down. Kevin as well of course, but I doubt he actually knows what's going on. Ever. Send me the new address as soon as you can, your letters are so far apart these days that I lose track of what we were talking about! A new address for a New Year is sort of fitting, don't you think?

Chloe and I are definitely, officially together now. Like, for sure. I finally just asked her about it, and she said she wasn't sure either, but we've cleared it up now. We've been out a lot together recently, and I've even met her family. I actually stayed at her house the other week – though grandma and grandpa don't know that yet. I would say it's definitely a real thing now. We've had to take a break from rehearsals for the play because of the school holidays, but it's been great that we are both in it because we have been able to practice our lines together. I think I am starting to get a grip on Shakespeare now too. Just in time!

I can't help but notice that you completely ignored my question about how you faked your death. Again. Every time I bring it up you seem to find a way to avoid answering it, I know it can't be something that you want to talk about particularly, but it is something that I am really curious about. Just explain it to me once so that I can put it out of my mind. Surely it would be good for you to talk about it as well. It must have been hard for you to do it, so maybe the best thing would be to get it off your chest. Does Samantha know that you did it yet? Please tell me.

Love,

Henry

Dear Henry,

Sam and I had a great Christmas and New Year, cheers. She says you're very welcome for the voucher, she's looking forward hearing what you end up spending it on. I'm made up you enjoyed the game. I was gonna try and surprise you and get a ticket myself, but in the end I couldn't justify taking the risk. Sorry about the result. It was a good one for us, like, but knowing that you were there I was hoping there'd be a few more goals for you and that. Happy New Year to you too, what else did Santa bring you for Christmas? You must be too old for all that now? I think I stopped believing in Santa when I was about 11.

Buzzing that you were all right with us moving in together. Everything is pretty sorted now with the new flat so I'll stick the new address at the end of this letter for you. Send your letters to the new one from now on though otherwise I won't ever get them, I'm giving the keys back over the weekend.

I'm made up for you and Chloe, mate. Good work, fella. It sounds like you two are having fun together, just watch it staying over and sneaking around behind your nan and granddad's back and that. You know what your nan is like, you don't want to be starting any kind of girl trouble in your house, mate. I've been there with her before, remember, she doesn't take it very well.

Not long until the play now, what dates in Feb is it on? Must be getting close, like, are you nervous yet? I'm sure you'll be sound on the lines by the time it rolls around, my mate. You're gonna boss it I'm sure. I was gonna ask you what character you're playing but then I realised it'd be pointless because I don't know any of them anyway. Maybe I'll give it a read before you perform, so I can talk to you about it properly.

Nothing gets past you, does it, fella? I have been ignoring it. I don't really want to have to talk about it. I know I'm going to one day but I wouldn't really know where to start to be honest. It's a bit of my past that I'm not dead keen on reliving. It's one of the few things I've ever done that I wish I could take back and do properly, so, you know, I'm not overly enthusiastic about talking through how I managed it, like. I tell you what, how about we address some things that you've ignored first? Once they've been dealt with then we can talk about how I faked my death, is that fair enough?

The first thing is that you promised to send me a picture of you. It's been a year now, or near enough, and I still haven't got a clue what you look like these days. While you're at it, send one over of Chloe, would be great to see the girl that finally managed to snag my lad's attention. Sam wants to see them as well.

The other thing is that we're into the New Year now, aren't we? I'm pretty sure that before Christmas we said we'd sort out meeting up sometime. Obviously you're dead busy at the moment with the play and that, so I don't expect it to be dead soon, but I don't want us to just keep forgetting about it and letting time go by when there's a chance we could be spending some of it together. How's it been going chatting through stuff with your nan? Has she opened up about me at all yet? Have you told her? If they're worried about how the meeting up will work and that, you can tell them that I'm sound to come up to you. I'll book a hotel and that so it's not dead awkward in the house or anything, and I'd only stay for a weekend or something the first few times, so it isn't too much hassle for them. Let me know, mate. I think we're definitely at the point where we should be giving it some thought, you know?

Love,

Robert (Dad)

P.S: The new address is:

> 92a Richmond Park Road,
> Queen's Park,
> Bournemouth,
> Dorset,
> BH8 8TQ

Dear Dad,

I am far too old for believing Santa is real now, yes.

Oh absolutely, it's amazing news that you'll be living together. I reckon you'll have to get used to watching less football now that your girlfriend is there all the time though – ha ha! Thanks for the new address, I hope this letter gets there okay, not that I suppose I would ever find out if it didn't! I looked up your new place on Google Maps; it is a bit further from the sea than your last house, but it's only about five minutes away anyway so it hardly matters. Don't go spending all of your time fishing and neglecting Samantha. Or Kevin, for that matter!

I know I shouldn't be sneaking around to see Chloe, but if grandma and grandpa had their way I might never get to spend any time with her outside school. Besides, her parents are fine with it so it's not like it's really hurting anybody. I don't exactly lie to grandma and grandpa about it, I just say that I am staying at a friend's house. It's technically true, if you think about it. You're right about grandma, the amount of lectures I have already had about, well, girls. They're both very awkward to talk to about stuff like that. She starts pretty well, and then it just turns into a 'back in my day' rant and I stop listening.

The play was amazing! It was on the Thursday, Friday and Saturday of Valentine's weekend. It was so much fun, but I was so, so, so nervous, especially on the first night. I was stood waiting to go on to do my first scene and Mr Lewton was standing there by the curtain as well, just watching how it was all going. I was talking to him really quietly, asking him what he thought of the audience and stuff, and I nearly missed my cue! I would have never gone on stage again if I had actually completely missed it, it would have been so embarrassing. As it happens, I realised just in time and I got all my lines right and everybody laughed at all the right bits. I think it went pretty well, to be honest. I only really had that one scene but it was worth it because it is such a rush when you are doing it. Grandma and grandpa said I was amazing, and they want me to do the next one. I can see why you enjoyed doing it so much now. I can't wait to do it again.

You know there isn't anything you can say that is going to upset me now, don't you? I've known you faked your death for a while, all I'm asking is you explain how. I'm more curious than anything else. But that's a fair deal, I think. I have sent a picture of me from sometime last year with this letter, so I do hope it reaches you okay. I wanted to send one of me in the show as well, but I don't have them yet so the other picture is of Chloe and me. It's from around Christmas time, so I doubt we have changed much since then. You can show Samantha them as well. Please send a picture of Samantha over with your next letter, I realised just the other day that I have no idea what she looks like. To think, you have moved in with this woman and all sorts and I still haven't said if she is pretty enough for you!

I think meeting up is a good idea too, but we would have to really talk about it and make sure that it worked well for us both. I'm sure that grandma and grandpa wouldn't mind you coming up to visit. I would have to ask them first though. If not, then I would probably have to convince them to let me go by myself. Perhaps once I've explained everything to them then they will be okay with it. She hasn't opened up much yet, but I haven't pushed it too much either. I've kept on with dropping hints about you, and I ask grandpa about you when we are by ourselves. I think it might be time to explain everything to them. I'll let you know how that goes...

Love,

Henry

Dear Henry,

You've got my ears. I knew it. Sam said it straight away as well. Aw mate I'm sorry about that, they've been a curse my whole life! Looks like you've grown up a handsome lad anyway, I dunno why you gave up playing footy. Looks like you've got the frame for it. I can't even begin to tell you what that felt like, fella. Seeing you after all these years. I know I haven't actually seen you yet, but like, that picture is something else. It's like working your whole life toward something that you never knew you'd even get to see, on the promise that you might. Then when you do, well, I can't explain it. A whole life that I never actually got to see being lived, never got to be a part of. Like someone was making me work on the wrong side of a door, and all the while you were growing up on the other side. Then I see that picture and it's a bit like you've just opened the door for the first time, and there we are, face to face. Only face to face with a picture of you, like, but there you were anyway. I stared at it for ages and then all I could say was 'yep, unlucky lad, they're my ears for sure'. I haven't seen you for 15 years, mate. Sorry if that all got a bit heavy for you. It's just weird, you know, you've gone from being a memory and a hope, to being words on a page. Now you're on the fridge door every time I go to make a cup of tea. Chloe is cute as well, mate, good work there. You've got good taste, just like your arl' fella!

No no no no no , there's still plenty of footy on our telly, mate. It was the first (and probably only) rule I had when we moved in – Sky Sports. Speaking of which, have you seen how well Bournemouth are doing this year? Mad, might actually be going up at this rate. Not looking so good for Burnley or Liverpool, like, but the less said about that the better.

The new flat is great, it is a bit further away from the water like, but I haven't had time to do any fishing yet anyway. Far too busy taking Kevin for walks down the beach, and taking Samantha for walks round IKEA. She can't get enough of that place, I swear. Plus, it's far too cold to be staying out all night fishing at this time of year, even if I only live down the road. Samantha has already said she's not interested in going with me until it warms up a bit, so I'm in no rush yet, like.

I'm made up the play went well for you, fella. That was a close call with your teacher though. Bang on for him to be distracting you that close to your cue, especially with it being your first show and that. It sounds like it went all right on the night. Great that your nan and granddad enjoyed it, I bet they're dead proud of you, like. I know that feeling you were on about, it's one that lasts for days as well. Like constant adrenaline racing through you, just makes everything you're doing seem so much more important and worthwhile, even if it's just something stupid like driving to work. Not that you do that, but I'm sure you know what I mean. It's like you've got this mad new purpose for doing everything, which is all great until it wears off. The post-show blues are the worst, especially if you enjoyed it as much as it sounds like you did. Can take a few days to shake them off, but it's a great reason to get straight back into it. That's what I was like at school, once I started I couldn't stop, fella, was hooked straightaway. Always played the dozy one, like. The clown or whatever.

Always acting the goat, but it was a right laugh.

Aw mate I can't say too much about this Chloe thing obviously, but I just think you're playing a dangerous game sneaking around your nan and granddad and that. I know it's awkward talking to them about it, but maybe if you were just honest with them they'd be better about it. Once it's all cleared up and out in the open it might make it easier to talk about staying with her or whatever, you know? Just be careful, mate. Also, I suppose I should say that, like, if you ever need to talk about any of that stuff properly, or if you've got, like, questions and that, or stuff you don't quite understand or know about yet, then you can ask me. I don't mind.

I didn't think it'd upset you to talk about it to be honest, mate. I just don't feel dead comfortable going through it all again. It's my problem really, but if you're that desperate to know then there's no reason not to tell you. I tell you what, you explain everything to your nan and granddad and sort out us meeting up. Once you've done that we'll set a date and then I'll explain everything to you beforehand. That sound good to you, fella? Ideally I wanted to come up and see you for your birthday, like, but I don't reckon that's gonna happen now. I'll stick a card in the post with some money in it for you or something. Make sure you get yourself something nice, or maybe have a day out with Chloe.

Love,

Dad

P.S: Might have some big news by the time you read my next letter!

Dear Dad,

I'm so glad that you liked the pictures I sent. I wasn't sure how you might react to seeing me after so long, but the way you put it was so funny and quite lovely. I'm honoured to be on your fridge door, you'll end up sick of the sight of me with the amount of tea you drink though. Thank you for what you said about Chloe, too; I'm glad you approve of her. You still forgot to send the picture of Samantha though!

So, I mentioned to grandpa Norman that I had been in contact with you. I thought it was about time, plus it's the best chance we have of meeting up, as you said. It took a long time for him to accept that you were still alive. He spent a while trying to comfort me about how you died and wasn't really listening. I told him that it wasn't quite as true as he thought and he kept asking how I knew you had faked it, which I was kind of lost on, obviously. I had to show him some of the letters before he would accept it was really you. We talked for a long time about you and what he remembered of you. I asked if he remembered the fishing incident when he went swimming after his rod and he laughed about that. He maintains that he never let you win at chess too, but I think he is still lying about that to make you feel better. I told him about how long we had been in contact for, which shocked him, but I was expecting that. He took it all quite well, actually. I asked him what he thought the best way to tell grandma would be, and he said that he would talk to her about it for me, which is a relief. Grandpa is okay with this sort of stuff, he kind of takes everything in his stride, you know? Grandma just panics about everything. Grandpa Norman said that once he has talked her round he can't see any reason that we wouldn't meet up, so that's good news. He stressed a lot about 'how did I know it was the real you' and blah blah blah, stranger danger and 'how this was like being safe online' and all of that rubbish. I just asked him how you would have known all that stuff about mum if it wasn't the real you. He doesn't think that it's a good idea for me to travel though, so that could be a problem if you can't come up here.

As it turns out, I also didn't have to talk about the Chloe thing with them either. Well, I did, but I didn't have to bring it up at least. Grandpa Norman took me to one side last week and just sort of launched into a conversation about girls and school and getting older and all that sort of thing. It was really weird and a bit awkward for him I think. I found it all quite funny to be honest, grandpa didn't want to say certain words in case, like, I don't know, he offended me or something, so I kept having to say them for him, as though I had never heard them before. It's nice that he did finally think to at least try and help me with that sort of thing, eventually. He mentioned that I might be wanting to stay over at Chloe's in the future (oops, ha ha) and that grandma might take a while to adjust to the idea, especially with how old we are. He made a point of stressing that even though I'm mature for my age, there's still no need to rush this sort of thing. Looks like I might just get away with it all after all. Don't you think it's funny how older people think that teenagers have never heard about or had sex, like old people invented it or something. They're always so awkward around it.

What's this big news all about? You can't say something like that in a 'PS' and then not tell me what it is, that just leaves everything on such a cliff-hanger. Make sure you don't forget to tell me about it, like you forgot the picture, or there will be big trouble!

I'm already looking forward to doing the next play with the school. Jack also mentioned that his cousin goes to a theatre group that is just outside Brindle, so I've asked Chloe if she wants to look into doing that with me as well. For once it was me asking her to do something, ha ha, she was shocked.

That's cruel on Samantha; if she doesn't like football you can't just make her watch it. I haven't really been keeping up much since we finished with the play, but I can't say that I'm surprised Burnley are doing so badly. After the game that Jack and I went to he said we weren't really good enough to compete in the Premier League anyway. Liverpool doing so badly is a surprise however, why do you think it is? I can't believe how well Bournemouth are doing. Do you think they actually have a chance of getting promoted this season? Would you go to the promotion party final thing?

Thank you very much for the card and the money! It was lovely of you to send something, but you really didn't have to. I haven't spent it yet, I'm never very good at deciding things I actually want!

Love,

Henry

Dear Henry,

That's amazing news about you telling your granddad everything. Made up he took it well, mate. I honestly had no idea how he would take it after so long. There was every chance he'd just flat out refuse to believe it, or just be furious with me for putting them through all of that. Sorry you didn't know how to answer when he asked how I had faked it, like. I did say I would tell you how I did it, and I will, I promise, eventually.

I think it's a great idea, you joining a youth theatre. I'm proud of you for just jumping into it like that. Hang on a second, you're giving your granddad grief for being old and talking about stuff like that, but aren't you a bit young for all that yet, like? He's right when he says you've plenty of time for all that. Don't blame your granddad for being awkward around sex, I'm a lot younger than him and I didn't even want to write it down. I think older people just have a hard time explaining it to people when they aren't sure how much you already know, if that makes any sense? You have to be sensitive about it obviously, it's just one of those things, isn't it? But seriously, mate, don't go being stupid or rushing anything either. There's a lot to be said for not growing up too quickly, I'm sure your nan and granddad would agree with me.

Don't worry about travelling to see me, I wasn't gonna let you do that anyway, mate. I'll come up to you. I'll come up in June. Is that okay? Let's say the middle of June for now, because that's far enough away for you to sort everything out with your nan and granddad and for me to book some proper time off work. I won't bring Sam with me the first time I come up. That reminds me, I wouldn't want to leave you on a 'cliff-hanger'. The big news I had was that I was thinking of proposing to Samantha, but I haven't done it yet. The timing wasn't quite right, and the night I was planning to do it she wasn't feeling very well, so I decided against it. I'll keep you updated and that, but I don't want you waiting in suspense. Anyway, I won't want waffle on too much because the quicker I get this one sent off to you the quicker we sort out a date and I can start getting excited about seeing you. Not sure I'll actually be able to believe it's real, meeting you again, like, until you're right there in front of me. Probably not even then. Let's say June 19th? That's what you can tell your nan and granddad and then they've got a date in their head that they can work toward as well. Tell them I'm dead easy with changing it and that if they want, but it gives them a chance to get themselves sorted out beforehand, chat to you about it, all of that stuff.

Let me know if that works for you all, fella.

Love,

Dad

Dear Robert,

Why haven't you proposed yet? Just do it! Don't tell me there's another chess game you have to win? You had better make it more romantic than your proposal to mum, too. That's really sweet though and I'm sure she will say yes. It's a shame you won't be bringing Samantha up to meet me but I understand, especially as it's the first time. Well, not the first time that we have met, but you understand what I mean.

I spoke to grandpa and grandma about it and they seem to think June 19th will be fine. They spent a long time talking about it though, I don't think they realised how quickly you wanted it all sorted out. Sorry about that. But yes, June 19th seems fine with them now, so I suppose that's all sorted. Will you come here then? Do you know the way? Maybe we should meet away from the house first, or would you rather grandma and grandpa are there when you arrive? I think they would probably prefer it that way, but I really don't mind. It might be easier for you to find your way to, I don't know, Blackburn or something, and I can meet you there. It's so soon, really, when you think about it. I'm very excited too but it is sort of scary, don't you think? I'm sure everything will be fine, but it's super strange.

Anyway, you made a promise to me and I don't want you to forget it or ignore it this time! The date is set; now you have to tell me how you faked it.

Love,

Henry

Dear Henry,

Made up that's all sorted. I can't wait, mate, I really can't. I did promise though, you're right, so here goes, I suppose.

The basics of it, mate, are that I made it look like a suicide. I knew that if it looked at any point like an accidental death, manslaughter, murder, anything like that, then there'd be a massive search on for who did it, and for where they'd hid my body. I didn't want to get anyone else into trouble, like, so I thought suicide was the best way to go. Besides, I had a good excuse, if you know what I mean? Your mum had just passed away and I had a baby to look after and had just lost my job as well, it all looked like stuff that might eventually, you know, push someone over the edge. I suppose it did in the end.

I made it look like we were going fishing, mate. Like I was taking the new little lad out for some quality father son time, and that I'd just decided to end it. Obviously there's planning that has to go into this sort of thing, like. From the day I decided it was my only option, I went into the bank bit by bit and withdrew everything we had left. I pay for everything in cash anyway usually so there wasn't anything dead suspicious about that. I left a bit in the account just so it wasn't obvious I was emptying it, and then bagged the rest up ready to go with me. I made sure that all the credit cards were in the wallet and I left them in the car. I thought about throwing my phone into the Mersey, but if it wasn't there when they found the car it would look a bit weird, so I left it. I'd already bought a bus ticket down to London and given them a fake name, which is dead easy because with certain companies you don't need ID or anything. Anyway, once that was all sorted out I had to think about what I was gonna do with you, you know? It wasn't safe to just leave you there without anyone knowing, so I had to make sure there was something in place or that someone was coming. We went down to the waterfront with the fishing gear, as I said, and I even half set up as though we were actually gonna do some fishing. You were still in your car seat. I spent about two hours with you, just sitting there making you smile and that, before I actually made a move. I made sure you would be warm enough, which was mad really because you were only gonna be there without me for about half an hour or so. I fed you your bottle, and then I just couldn't, you know. I had no idea how long it might be before I'd be able to see you again once I'd pressed the button on my phone and set it all in motion. You were falling asleep by the time I actually called your nanny Lynne. I wanted her and your granddad to be the first to find you so that they would be the ones that took you in first. I knew how much they loved you and that if they thought they were the only proper family you had left then they would never let you be taken anywhere else. I got that bit right, at least. I called her in tears, which I'd love to say was my acting experience coming through, mate, but it wasn't, I felt like I was actually, slowly dying with every word. I told her how it had all piled up and it was too much, and how I couldn't provide for you any more, but I knew that her and your granddad could. When she started worrying I told her where I was and told her to come and collect you. She said she'd be down straight away and that was it then, it was too late. That was my only chance. I very nearly didn't take it, as well. I sometimes wish I hadn't. I took off my coat and threw it in the Mersey, I thought if they found that then they'd be convinced that I had jumped in and that. Once I'd done that I made sure the car was unlocked and left the key on the pavement next to it. That's the reason I was sure she never liked me, if I'm honest, mate. It was cruel, to call her like that. I'd be amazed if she ever got over it.

Once I had done all of that I just started walking down the prom, in the opposite direction to the one I knew your nan would be coming from. I walked most of the way backwards, so that I could keep an eye on the car with you in it, like, in case anyone else tried to get to you before your nan did. Once I got too far to see properly I stood at one of them mad blue telescope things you get on promenades, you might have seen them when you went to Blackpool? I just kept sticking 20ps in it until I had watched your nan arrive and then saw the flashing lights of the police, and that was that. I knew once they arrived I had to get as far away as I could. I kept walking until I reached a bus stop, then just got on a random series of buses, really. Whichever one was going furthest away, I think. I would just get on and ride to the end of the line. I think I thought if I didn't know where I was going, then it would be impossible to follow me. I ended up somewhere near Crewe. I asked about homeless shelters, and there was one that wasn't too far away. That was home for about a week, until I reckoned they would have stopped looking for me and that. I sat in that room all week, surrounded by strangers, and just cried. It must have looked nuts. There was nothing else I wanted to do, mate. The reality of what I had done was starting to sink in. It's amazing, the stuff that you realise you can't do any more. Can't log in to anything online, can't use any kind of phone or sim card or anything like that, can't really use a computer full stop. Can't call mates or let anyone know you're okay. I struggled to even see the matches that were on. Being that close to home I didn't want to risk getting recognised in pubs or anything, so unless I was feeling particularly brave I didn't watch them. I ended up missing my bus to London, I hadn't really thought it through. I'd booked the ticket from Liverpool, but obviously I was nowhere near by the day that it was leaving. I went by train instead, just little journeys at a time. I had enough money to get me right down to London, which was where I knew I'd be able to find a bit of cash in hand work, just to see me through for a bit, like. I got my hair dyed and started growing a beard, then I started labouring for a plasterer who was doing contract work for housing estates round Brixton. He wasn't allowed to have anyone subcontracted to him, technically, so it worked out dead well for him as well, the cash in hand thing. I told him that I was just a kid looking for a fresh start and he didn't ask too many questions, thankfully. Mickey, his name was. Well, actually his name was Joseph, but he hated that and all of his mates called him Mickey, so that's what I called him as well.

I did about 3 months with Mickey before I had enough to move on. I had planned to just go online and order a dodgy fake driving license or something, you know, off one of them blag websites you can get IDs from. But obviously I had no bank account, so I couldn't pay for anything online anyway, and I had nowhere to get it delivered too. I had to start small, taking out memberships for loyalty cards and that sort of thing. Eventually I found a gym I could get a membership for and kept telling the woman on the desk

I'd bring my ID in next time. Just trying to build up a bit of a paper trail, you know? That's when I picked out James Rayner, as my new name I mean. Getting a bank account was the hardest bit, but I knew once I had that sorted I was sound. I won't bore you with it, like, but it was a lot of photocopied fake IDs and trying to pick out the doziest looking bank clerk.

Once it was finally done I put all the money I had left in the account, thanked Mickey for his help and moved out of London. There was nowhere I really wanted to go, so I thought I'd give Bournemouth a go, seeing as it was on the coast and that. I was in and out of dodgy hotel rooms, hostels, that sort of thing, then I managed to bunk in with some students down there for a bit who were subletting a room without their landlord knowing about it. I took work doing whatever, anything that wasn't asking for National Insurance, because obviously that was the big one that I didn't have, like. I managed to get hold of a flat to rent from this old woman, proper coffin dodging, she was, looked like she'd been cheating death for the past 300 years. She agreed to me paying the rent straight into her bank account, which was sound. I stayed there and worked pretty much full time then, doing whatever. Mostly building work, to be honest, as people seem happy to pay in cash for that. I spent ages dodging the tax man and then I thought I'd have a look, see what was involved in getting National Insurance or whatever. Turns out that if you can prove you've lived in the UK the Jobcentre will take care of most of it for you, so I thought I'd see how far I got. It took ages, loads of questions and interviews and asking about ID and that. Eventually, I'm not really sure how, it was pushed through and I was told that I could tell employers I'd applied for National Insurance, and that I was just supposed to tell them when it arrived. It still hasn't! Someone must have realised somewhere down the line that I wasn't eligible but they never called me up on it, like, so that's what I did. Started applying for jobs telling them it was on its way. That's how I ended up where I am now. I started working for Bournemouth Computer Solutions, which is where I met Samantha. She wasn't there long but we stayed in touch, like. Well, you knew that bit. That was that really, mate. The rest I suppose you've already heard about or can figure out. I never thought, stood at that car window looking at you for what could have been the last time, that I'd be able to pull it off. I thought I'd end up getting cold feet and coming back to you, getting caught and banged up for fraud or something. I just had to take it one day at a time, like, keep plodding along and hoping that eventually it would all sort itself out.

I never thought it actually would, but here we are. Now I'm a few weeks away from meeting you again, making up for all them lost years. All those matches we could have been watching together. You might even have learned how to properly set your fishing tackle up by now and all. You'd definitely have been a Liverpool fan. But there's plenty of time for that now. I can't wait to see you, mate. I hope you can understand a bit of what I went through now, after I left you and that. It was actually good to get it off my chest after all these years, to be honest.

I'll see you soon, my mate. (I say that, you're not so little any more).

Love,
Dad

Dear Mr Henderson, or Mr Rayner,

I am entirely unsure how best to approach this most delicate situation. My name is Joanne Dagnall, and I believe that for the past eighteen months, give or take, you have been in regular contact with my granddaughter, Alice. If I am correct, then this will come as quite a surprise to you, and I am very sorry that I am the one that has to inform you. I am writing this letter to you to attempt to make a little more sense of the situation, but also to allay any confusion around what has happened. Alice came to me in quite a state last week, aware that you expected to be meeting her very soon. Perhaps it would be more accurate to say that you expected to be meeting your son, but Alice was upset by the ordeal nonetheless. You can imagine my surprise, and, initially, horror, at the prospect that my granddaughter was set to meet a middle-aged man who she didn't really know.

Having heard the details of your correspondence only last week, it is difficult for me to fully comprehend the scale of the sense of disappointment and, to a point, betrayal, which you must feel. I would ask, however, that you consider Alice's role in all of this before you cast your judgement. From what I have gathered from your letters, Alice is a girl in a similar position to your son. She never knew her father, which I believe is the reason she was so keen to impersonate your son in the first place. She yearns for that paternal connection that she has never quite established with her grandfather. Her mother works hard, but in her role she is required to travel an awful lot. As a result, Alice lives, for the majority of the year, with her grandparents – my husband and myself. When your first letter arrived through the door it was Alice found it. She is a naturally curious girl and, knowing that nobody by the name of Henry lived at this address, she decided to open the letter. I think she identified with your son and his situation. It resonated with her and compelled her to reach out. I believe that it was that same inquisitive nature of hers that led her to impersonate Henry. At first she genuinely believed that she was doing a good thing, that your letter didn't deserve to be ignored and that it would mean so much to you to receive a response. There was no malice or ill will in her actions, just the intrigue of a teenage girl who had found a comforting voice. A diary that spoke back to her, if you will.

You became so much more to her than that, however, Mr Henderson. She confided in you details of her schooling and personal situations that her grandfather and I were entirely unaware of. I believe that the 'Chloe' referred to in her letters are self-referential. There is certainly a striking similarity between Chloe and Alice's situations. The issues that Chloe battled with in school are the same issues that Alice has faced for a long, long time. It may be a worthless assertion, especially as she has no real connection to your situation at all, but know that you have helped Alice immeasurably. You instilled a sense of confidence in her, the likes of which I have never seen before. I should have suspected there was something going on when she began to express an interest in fishing and football: they are both things that have never really had much of a place in our household. Her grandfather obliged her whenever he could, but we were both left scratching our heads at times at her sudden zeal for such hobbies. She is, as I gather, around a year or two older than Henry is. She was fifteen years old when you first made contact, and at her next birthday will be seventeen. These crucial formative years have been made so much easier for her having you to talk to, to bounce her insecurities off a complementary and soothing voice. She did take up theatre, inspired by you, and I have never seen such a change in her. It brought her out of herself, and we have you to thank for that entirely. We had no idea that she was being so harassed and bullied by older girls in her school. Of course, had we known, we would have intervened, but your advice and guidance throughout has helped her to move past it. She has matured so much, and grown into a fine young woman who is as sure of herself as you and I. You have given her that.

I must admit, there were even moments of relief as I read through your correspondence. Her thinly veiled references to her own experiences with alcohol and sex are issues that I fear she would simply never raise with my husband or myself. It was a growing concern for us both that she could become involved with such things without having been properly educated on them. It is perhaps our own failings as her guardians that led us to such a worry, but you have helped her immensely with understanding that there is no rush, no pressure to have these experiences for their own sake, at least not until she feels comfortable doing so. Having never discussed these matters with her before, it was a milestone in our relationship when she came to me for advice regarding her current situation. It was the first time that we had ever talked so openly about her personal life, and our relationship is blossoming as a result. Again, Mr Henderson, I have you to thank for that.

There must be a thousand questions that you would like to ask about all of this. I will do my best to answer as many of them as I can. Please feel free to contact me, or indeed Alice, with any concerns. The photograph that she sent you of 'Henry and Chloe' is in fact a picture of Alice and her cousin, taken over the Christmas period. The reason that she became so short and frustrated when you broke the news of your girlfriend was, I believe, because she had become rather attached to you. Easily done for an impressionable teenage girl, but I believe there was a hint of jealousy and betrayal at the thought that you, who had become such a father figure to her, were spending so much time with another woman. You paid Alice attention; you were always so pleased to speak to her and gave so much time to the communications. It's the first time in her life that she had experienced such a mature connection, so we can forgive her inexperience and attachment, I think. She was in the school's recent production of A Midsummer Night's Dream at the school. My husband, Alex, and I both attended, as did her mother. We have never been so proud. Her mother cried at the close of the production, and was at a complete loss for words. The reason it took Alice so long to reveal the extent of your correspondence to me was because she was unsure how to undo what she had already done. From the moment she sent the first letter it became increasingly difficult for her to explain that what she was doing was dishonest. I maintain, however, that while it was intentionally deceptive of her, it was not malevolent. It was a safe illusion for her for a long time, or so she thought. Until you started to speak of meeting her for the first time she had never really considered the implications for you. It is, and was, incredibly selfish of her, of course, to take away so much time that you could have spent, and indeed that you believed you had spent, building a relationship with your son.

I have to say, Mr Henderson, that I find your situation truly remarkable. While it is not my place to judge, especially without full knowledge of your circumstances, I believe that your somewhat drastic actions were performed for the right reasons. You had the interests of your son at heart, and that is most commendable. I hope you don't mind me saying so. I also desperately hope that you are able to connect with your son, and that this confusion has not put you off the idea. It is on this subject that I think I may at least be able to offer you some form of recompense for the time that you must feel you have wasted. Your letters were incorrectly addressed, a fact I'm sure you now realise. As an attempt to thank you for all you have done for Alice, I have taken the liberty of researching the address that you intended the letters for. I have met your son. I have met his grandfather, Norman, who is still very much an avid fisherman. His grandmother, Lynne, and I used to attend the same community choir. The address you want is as follows:

Stoney Bank,
Sandy Lane,
Brindle,
Chorley,
Lancashire,
PR6 8NL

I hasten to add that the above is now also a useless address for your purposes, however. The family moved away from Brindle some years ago now, hence the need for research on my part. I managed to obtain their new address for you, which is as follows:

The Old Posting House,
62 Speen Lane,
Speen,
Newbury,
RG14 1RN

Naturally I expect that Alice will hear far less of you now that you are able to connect with your son. I do wish you all the luck in the world with Henry, and I hope you are able to reconcile your issues with the family. If you can establish anything like the relationship you forged with Alice, then I daresay everything will work out for you in the end.

Again, Mr Henderson, I can only apologise for what must be an absolute bombshell for you and your (hopefully, by now) intended. Congratulations to you both, by the way. This all began with a young girl who needed somebody to talk to. She never considered how it might impact on your situation, and for that too, I must apologise profusely on her behalf. But I must also thank you, Mr Henderson. You provided her with the support that she needed, you saw her through some of the most difficult times and situations that she has faced. We are eternally grateful for the effect that your continued kind words have had on her development and her confidence. She has grown from a timid, troubled teenager to an assured young woman, all thanks to you. Though it may mean little to you in light of these events, Alice owes an awful lot to you that she could never possibly repay. Thank you, Mr Henderson. I am hoping with all of my heart that you can experience some of the same revelations that you have brought for us, with your own son.

I have enclosed the picture of your late wife and yourself with this letter, as well as the image of your lovely dog. Alice has taken copies of them, as she is keen to remember your influence, but I informed her that it would be cruel to retain the original. I hope you don't mind. Before penning this letter, she made me promise that I would emphasise how hopeful she is that some form of correspondence between you both can continue. I leave that to you.

Yours gratefully, and forever apologetically,

Joanne, Alex and Alice Dagnall

Dear Henry,

It'll be fifteen years this week since I last saw you. A lot has changed for us both in that time, I reckon. My name is Robert Henderson, which you might have already heard. I'm your dad. Your real dad. This is bound to all be dead confusing for you, but despite what you've probably been told about me, I'm not dead. I never meant for it to take this long to get in touch with you, I really didn't, mate, but I can explain all that in good time. It's a weird little story, but I think you'll like it.

The first thing I'll say is Happy Birthday, fella. It's been a long time coming, like, and I'm so sorry I've never managed to get in touch with you before now. Trust me when I say I never wanted things to work out like this, but I'll explain a bit of it, anyway.

You were born on 8th March 2000. Best and worst day of my life, that was. Your mum passed away while she was giving birth to you. Nobody ever blamed you for it, mate. These things happen sometimes, you know? She experienced what is called PPH minutes after she gave birth. I won't go into the details of it, 'specially not round your birthday, but that was how she went. Jess was her name, but like, you probably already know all about her from your nan and granddad. She was gorgeous. My best mate for years and then we ended up together and then we ended up married and having you, it was all a bit of a whirlwind when we were younger like, but it was good fun. Funny thing is we weren't even meant to be having you. We hadn't long been married and then we found out. Not like you were an accident, we just weren't expecting her to get pregnant, if that makes sense? It didn't matter anyway, from the second I found out I couldn't wait. I didn't even know you were gonna be a boy. Your mum told the doctors we wanted it to be a surprise and that, but I knew you'd be my little lad. Funny how you just know some things, isn't it?

So anyway, after your mum passed away it was just me and you for a bit, back in our little flat on Mulgrave Street. It was hard, fella. It was really hard. I was working as an electrician with Robshaw's at the time and I didn't really handle losing your mum well so I didn't tell the bosses there. I didn't tell them I wanted any time off and I kept trying to go to work, took you with me on a few jobs and that, even though your car seat didn't really fit properly in the van, like. I couldn't have you with me all the time though, and obviously I thought your mum was gonna be there to look after you, so it got hard to stay on top of everything. I kept missing jobs and skipping call outs to look after you or drop you at your nan and granddad's house before work, but they could only have you some of the time. I didn't want to kick up a fuss so just told the bosses I was having a bit of a hard time with stuff and I'd try and pick it up. I couldn't, and you ended up spending more time with your nan and granddad than with me. They saw your first smile while I was in the estate agents arguing over missed rent. I was dropping you off one day, going up their driveway with you in the van next to me, and it just sort of came to me that you might be better off there. Permanently I mean. I was suspended that morning and that was like the tipping point, you know? I knew there were no other jobs going anywhere, and we were living on less and less each day. Your nan and granddad were great, like, and they helped out wherever they could and offered to pay some of the bills, but I could just see that they were so disappointed, like I wasn't ready to be a dad yet, and it was ripping me apart, mate. It wasn't your fault you had a skint dad who couldn't look after you, and you deserved better, so I started planning. I faked my own death so that you could stay with your nan and granddad full time. They had everything that we didn't and I knew they would be able to take care of you. I know it sounds drastic, mate, it was, but I couldn't face watching you grow up from the sidelines while I was struggling to pay bills and you were missing out on all the things I wanted to do with you as a kid. As dad and lad, like it was meant to be. I couldn't take the shame of you growing up knowing you had a dad who couldn't sort his life out. I didn't want you to be disappointed by me. It was desperate, and I was a coward about it, but it was the easiest way to give you everything I wanted you to have.

It tore me apart, leaving you. I'm so sorry, mate. Sorry that you've had to live all this time thinking your dad was dead. Sorry for not being around in the first place. I'm sorry that I've had to send this letter after all this time, to turn everything upside down for you again. This time, at least, I hope it can be for the better. I'm not expecting you to forgive me, I wouldn't be offended if you never forgave me. I wouldn't blame you if you never wanted to speak to me, mate, but I had to let you know. To let you know that your dad was still here, still thinking of you all the time. I've wanted to talk to you every day since I left, and now I've finally got that chance. I hope that you can bring yourself to reply to this letter. I was a coward, mate, I really was, but if you can see fit to give me another chance to prove that I only ever did what I did so that you could have a real chance at a good life, then we can fix it together. It was a chance at a life that I would never have been able to give you. I wasn't ready to be a good dad the first time around, I had to find that out the hard way, like. I know I can do a better job of it this time.

If you do want to talk, send a letter to this address:

92a Richmond Park Road,
Queen's Park,
Bournemouth,
Dorset,
BH8 8TQ

Hope to hear from you soon, mate.

Happy birthday, little man.

Love,

Robert

ACKNOWLEDGEMENTS

My thanks go to: Robert Peett, Cat Hall, Yen-Yen Lu, Natasha Robson, Tracey Green, Simon Wray, Ciara Durnford, Peter Robinson, Dan Meigh, Stewart Jones, Samantha Morrish, Charlie Coleman, Mat Oliphant, Stuie Dagnall, Beryl Green, Mickey Green, Lenny Wray, Ryan Wray, Lauren Wray, Lily Wray, Slevin, Off the Ground Theatre and Infinite 3D

Lightning Source UK Ltd.
Milton Keynes UK
UKOW02f0912150916

283039UK00002B/10/P